Wanted

S. Nelson

Wanted/ S.Nelson. -- 1st edition

ISBN-13: 978-1514808917

ISBN-10: 1514808919

I dedicate this book to my sister Pam. I can't thank you enough for all of your continued love and support as I follow my dream. You've been there through every single stage of this new journey, encouraging me along the way. You were the first person to read my first book, and even though the rough draft is still sitting on your bookcase, I know you won't show it to anyone. LOL. Can you believe this is the end of the trilogy? And my fifth book? It's so crazy yet wonderfully amazing. I love you and can't wait until I have another story for you to delve into. ☺

~1~

Sara

I woke up with the worst headache I'd had in a long time. It'd been years since I felt that way—eight years, to be exact.

Knowing the previous few hours weren't a nightmare, everything came crashing over me like a tidal wave.

The parking lot.

Brian being hit in the head and toppling forward.

Me on the ground.

Then looking into the face of the one man who turned my sweet, innocent life upside-down. The one man I'd tried to block from the deepest recesses of my mind.

Samuel Colden.

He was there in the dark, stifling room with me. I could sense it from the way my body reacted, an innate fear radiating through every cell of my trembling body.

How long have I been here? Where did he take me? Will anyone find me this time?

All those years before, it took the authorities nine long, agonizing, torturous days to find me, and they'd been informed Samuel was the last person to see me. He was identified as giving me a ride, for Christ's sake. And it *still* took them that long to rescue me.

How long would it take for someone to come save me this time? There in Seattle, if I was even still there, left it wide open for the possibilities of where he could be keeping me. It would be so much harder this time around.

The longer I laid there, the more I seemed to drift in and out of consciousness. I tried to will myself to stay awake for longer than five minutes at a clip, but my body had other ideas.

Unfortunately, I could remember exactly all the feelings I was going through and, oddly enough, with lucid clarity.

I remembered the headaches, the aches from where I was being restrained, the fading in and out of blackness and the utter fear. Fear which traveled throughout my entire body, my soul even.

I didn't know how long I'd been there, waiting for something else to happen, anything to happen. I didn't want to succumb to what I undoubtedly feared Samuel was going to do to me, but I didn't want to prolong it for endless hours...days even. If he was going to kill me, I would rather he do it and stop torturing me.

I heard his shoes scuffing the wood boards above my head.

I heard the jingle of keys.

Then I heard the door open and heavy steps descend the creaky stairs.

Darkness surrounded me like a blanket of despair while I waited for Samuel to make his move.

The area I was being held in had to be some sort of room hidden in the basement. The dank, musty smell was a tell-tale sign. He was smart enough to know he would be in more danger of being caught if he held me on one of the main floors.

So many questions raced through my head. Was the house abandoned? Did he rent the place, waiting for the opportunity to snatch me up? Was he watching me? If so, for how long?

The biggest question afflicting me was what were his plans for me this time?

It was then I heard short, rapid breaths hitting the shell of my ear. Instantly, my own breathing quickened and goose bumps broke out all over my skin, giving me a feeling of pure dread.

"I've missed you so much, Sara. You're all I thought about when I was locked away. I told you I never wanted to go back, but you made me." His fingers slid along my jaw. "You made me go back there, Sara," he repeated.

To drive home his complaint, he gripped my hair and painfully yanked my head to the side, making me cry out.

"Please, Samuel. Please, don't do this to me." I trembled, unable to control the shakes which had taken over my body. "I want to go home. Please, just let me go home."

"To him?" A question at first. Although, the next time he spoke, it was a statement. "You want to go home to him."

"Please," I begged. I knew better than to mention Alek. Knowing it would enrage him further, I did my best to keep off-topic from the man he apparently already knew about.

"I saw you with him, Sara. I saw you kiss him. Hold his hand. I saw you hug him." His hot breath fanned my face. "It should have been me. But you sent me away. And now, you must pay for your sins. Pay for every one of them."

The man before me wasn't the same man from eight years ago. Yes, he was crazy, certifiably out of his mind. But the Samuel from long before wouldn't have wanted to punish me so. He simply wanted to be with me. We were involved in some sort of twisted—albeit normal, in his mind—relationship.

He'd certainly had enough time over the years to dream up all sorts of ways for making me pay for what he thought I did to him. In his warped brain, I was to blame for having him locked up in the nut house.

With his acknowledgment of Alek, there was no doubt in my mind he thought I'd been cheating on him. What was his punishment going to be for my infidelity? I had to derive some sort of argument when he broached the subject again.

I had to think like a crazy person. What words would satisfy the insane?

"What are you going to do to me?" Maybe I should have thought about the possible answer to my question before I asked it. Sometimes ignorance *was* bliss, especially in a case such as mine.

I had everything to live for, more so than when he'd stolen me before. I had great friends and had finally found the man of my dreams. A man who was never going to hear me tell him I loved him. A man who would forever blame himself for whatever Samuel was going to do to me.

I knew how much Alek tried to protect and keep me safe. My abduction was going to destroy him. Even if he found me, the damage was irrevocable. Knowing how much he'd sacrificed over the years to see to it no harm came to me, Samuel had destroyed his security in the blink of an eye.

My captor shuffled across the room, ruffling through drawers and tossing things around. When he was finished, he made his way back up the stairs, never answering the question I'd asked him.

Waiting was the one thing which was going to unravel me. Obviously, I didn't want him to harm me, but there was no telling how long he would drag out the anticipation for what was to come.

The more time I had to contemplate my new fate, all sorts of scenarios running rampant inside my head, the more my reality drifted away from me.

And I needed to be in the present if I was going to have any chance of survival.

~2~

Sara

I woke up to the side of my face being smacked. At first it was light, then when I'd still not opened my eyes, it was sharp and painful.

"Wake up, Sara," Samuel said as soon as he knew his slap had done the trick of bringing me back to my twisted reality. He hovered over me, his body close to mine as he tested the restraints, making sure they were still intact.

The more my consciousness took over, the more I realized I really needed to use the restroom. My poor bladder hadn't been empty in I had no idea how long. *How long have I even been here?* Would he loosen the chains or would he make me use a bed pan like last time?

I'm about to find out.

"Samuel, I have to go to the bathroom. Can you please untie me?"

"No," was all he said.

"Please," I begged. "I don't want to make a mess all over myself. I'll be quick, I swear."

His tone became more agitated the more I pushed him to respond. "I know if I untie you, you're going to try and escape." He'd walked across the small space and was rustling through an old, beat-up drawer. Earlier, he'd brought a small lamp down with him, which allowed me to see what he was doing. "You've only been here five hours and you already want to leave me." Slamming the drawer shut, he turned toward me and shouted, "You want to leave me and go back to him!" His fists were clenched at his sides and I knew better than to push him when he was so lost in his delusion. "But you can't. I won't allow it. I won't lose you again." His last few words were barely spoken above a whisper, and they were more haunting than the ones he shouted.

My thoughts were immediately overrun by the people in my life. My best friend Alexa who would be beyond worried about me, knowing the whole story of my past; Matt, who had recently learned of what had happened to me all those years ago; and Alek, the one person who had tried to save me, even from myself sometimes.

If what Samuel had said was true and I had only been missing for five hours then Alexa and Matt might not even know yet. But there was no doubt Alek knew. I would never *not* show up, especially not without at least contacting him. He was forever reminding me to charge my phone and make sure I kept the ringer on, but even then, I would have found a way to call him.

Regret suddenly gripped me from the inside. Damn it! I should have never ditched Brian. Even though he eventually found me, he had been distracted, so worried about what Alek would have done to him had he not caught up with me. If I'd done what I was supposed to then my shadow would have been aware of our surroundings, cutting Samuel off as he approached or even securing me so well, he would have never even shown himself.

Damn my stubbornness and need to always go against Alek's warnings.

A noise to my right pushed me from my thoughts, and it was then I realized my need to go to the bathroom had only intensified. I heard shuffling across the floor before the groan of the step. *My bladder muscles are going to be tested. I hope they're up for the challenge.*

I wasn't quite sure how much time had passed until he came back down to the basement. He quickly approached me, scaring me enough to cause me to flinch. The scowl on his face told me he didn't appreciate my reaction. Reaching forward, he unbound my hands from the posts above my head but left the restraints around my ankles. My poor limbs screamed when I lowered them, soreness and the rush of blood causing me to wince and moan in discomfort.

Before I knew what was happening, he lifted me from the old mattress and instantly bound my hands behind my back. He was making sure I wasn't going to try and escape. I stumbled as he ushered me toward the toilet in the corner of the room. It wasn't a far walk, but the chains around my ankles made it near impossible to take a steady step.

As I opened my mouth to ask him how he expected me to go to the bathroom without the use of my hands, his fingers flew to the button on my jeans, yanking them down along with my underwear. Mortified, I turned my head to the side and held my breath. Gripping my shoulders, he pushed me down until I sat on the toilet seat.

Thankfully, Samuel had not sexually assaulted me the first time he kidnapped me. But would this time be different? Had his fascination grown over the years he was locked away? I shuddered at the thought and prayed he wouldn't have enough time to even contemplate such an act.

My body didn't care what havoc was swirling around inside my brain. Once I sat on the toilet, my bladder sighed in relief. In truth I should've been thankful he hadn't made me use a bedpan like before. Although humiliating, this was a bit more dignified.

Once finished, I tried my best to stand on my own, but it was more difficult than I'd imagined.

Witnessing my struggle, he immediately grabbed my arms to help steady me. He reached for a nearby rag and pressed it against me, drying me before he pulled my underwear and jeans back up. There was nothing sexual in his eyes or touch when he wiped me, even though his hand was essentially covering my most intimate place.

My stomach revolted from his touch, though. I had to take a deep breath to make sure I didn't throw up all over myself.

Leading me back toward the bed, he gently placed me on the old mattress and made quick work of reattaching my chains. His actions were gentle, telling me he didn't really wish to cause me harm. Maybe I was reading too much into a simple gesture, but it was all I had. It gave me hope, and I would clutch on to it for as long as it remained true.

He disappeared from the room only to return not long after, carrying a bowl of food which smelled pretty good. Fortunately, I had the sense to know he'd probably drugged it and thankfully, I was nowhere near starvation.

The bed dipped from his weight. I stared into his eyes, trying to see if I could gauge anything, trying to catch a glimmer of what was to come. But there was nothing. His vacant stare was glazed over, as if he wasn't even present.

His eyes locked on mine so long I would have sworn we were engaged in some sort of contest. Finally, he broke the silence with his gruff voice.

"I'm sure you're hungry, Sara. I brought you beef stew." When I didn't make a move or respond, he pushed the spoon closer to my mouth, letting a small amount of it hit my chest as it fell from the utensil.

It was lukewarm at best.

My lips locked up tight and I tried my best to shake my head. I didn't want to anger him, but I didn't trust I wouldn't fall sick because of what he was trying to feed me.

As I struggled to back away, he reached forward and painfully gripped my chin, pulling me closer. Prying my lips open with his dirty fingers, he slipped the spoon inside my mouth.

I instantly started coughing, spitting out the small amount of stew he'd managed to feed me. But he kept at it, shoveling the warm food past my lips. Because I had no other choice, I swallowed a portion of it. It was either eat or choke to death.

I chose to stay alive another day.

After he was done, he simply disappeared back upstairs, leaving me alone yet again to ponder how long my future would be.

~3~

Alek

It'd been two of the longest days of my fucking life. The tracker I'd installed on Sara's phone right after I found out Samuel was released kept fading in and out. She had no idea I'd put the damn thing on there, but I was sure it would be the one and only time she wouldn't argue with me about invading her privacy.

I'd also placed a device on her car, but finding the vehicle abandoned in a busy parking lot was a huge setback. But had I really thought it would have been easy?

The need for discretion was of the utmost importance because I didn't want to alert Samuel, fearing he would move her, taking her away from me forever. Every time I'd been close to where I thought she was kept, it was a false alarm.

Thankfully, I had many connections and a lot of people who owed me favors. Calling in one such service, I'd had a local realtor run the names of all the people who'd either purchased or rented a place within a hundred-mile radius of Seattle. I knew it was a long shot, but I was hoping he'd taken her somewhere nearby.

Taken.

I still couldn't believe he'd been able to snatch her away from me so easily. Thinking I'd taken every precaution, I'd gotten lazy. I should have been with her. Twenty-four-fucking-seven. No one could protect her like I could, or so I'd thought.

Guess I was wrong.

I prayed I could make things right again, bring Sara back home and dispose of Samuel once and for all. What did that mean exactly? I had no idea. I figured we'd see how things panned out, but I wasn't above getting my hands dirty in order to secure her very long, bright future.

None of the property searches turned up anything, so I'd have to go off the unreliable tracker. Its signal waned the further north of the city I drove, leading me to a more generalized area.

Driving around side streets without my headlights proved to be treacherous. The dark of the night threatened to swallow me up if I wasn't careful. It was funny because if I'd really thought I lost her forever, I would have run screaming into its steely cold embrace.

But I had hope.

Never mind my intuition was heightened. The chemistry which typically flowed between us was faint, but still present.

As I traveled down a dead-end street, there was a house on the corner which looked to be abandoned. The roof was old, shingles hanging off the sides, threatening to fall off given one more rainstorm. The front porch was missing and the siding was rotting away, as if whatever was housed inside had caused all the damage.

Instinct told me she was there. Plus the tracker suddenly picked up a stronger signal.

I ended up two hours outside of Seattle. *So much for her being close by.* Although, I would drive to the ends of the Earth if it meant I would find her, bring her home with me where she'd be safe and away from Samuel. I couldn't even imagine what she was going through. To be taken...twice...by the same man. The fear she must've been experiencing was enough to reduce me to tears.

Fighting back the lump in my throat, I knew I had to be strong. I had to search, hopefully find her inside the decaying house and get the hell out.

Quickly.

Parking down the road, I gently closed my car door. I steadily crept along, trying as much as I could to stay hidden behind whatever shelter I could find. Trees, shrubs, vehicles parked along the street— they were all the camouflage I needed right then.

With every step I took, I prayed she was still breathing. I didn't think he would kidnap her only to kill her right away. Although I was trying my best to see things through his eyes, I simply wasn't hard-wired as a mad man.

When I finally came upon the house, it was eerily quiet. There was but one light on, in the back, toward what was probably the kitchen.

It was all I needed.

Creeping along the side, I searched for a basement. I didn't know why my mind went there but it did. Maybe it was all those damn scary movies Sara made me watch. I much preferred action flicks, but if her insistence on the horror genre was what eventually led me to her, then I would watch each and every one she wanted from there on out.

As I stood there, my thoughts overtook me. Dark thoughts. Hopeless thoughts. I'd envisioned what my life would be like without the infuriating, amazing and beautiful woman who had come crashing into it.

That sort of fate I wouldn't survive. I would be but a shell of a man. At least before, I had no idea what I'd been missing out on. But now...there was no going back.

For as much as I wanted to spend the next fifty years of my life cherishing, arguing with, and loving her, I couldn't shake the feeling I was doing more harm than good being so involved in her life.

In all the years I'd committed to protecting her, watching her and staying in the background, her safety was never once compromised. But ever since I'd made the selfish decision and invited myself into her world, up-close and personal, she'd been put in two very dangerous situations.

First, the creep at Carlson's who attacked her in the hallway, and then Samuel kidnapping her again.

Pushing my uncertain thoughts to the back of my mind, I knew I didn't have time to contemplate what it all meant. Sara was still in grave danger and with every second that passed, I ran the risk of losing her forever.

When I'd snuck around to the back of the house, I cautiously tried to peer through every available window, but it was of no use because they were heavily shaded from the inside. I decided to try the back door, praying it wasn't heavily barricaded. When my fingers circled the handle, it turned. But the door didn't open.

As quietly as I could, I hit the frame with my shoulder. It was loud at first, especially since it was the only sound drifting through the air around me. I hit it again. Finally, the wood splintered and the door flung open. I caught it before it hit the wall inside.

I'm pretty good at breaking down doors, it seems.

As I stepped over the threshold, I was bombarded with thoughts of an ambush. Did he know I was there? Was he waiting for me?

Moving three more steps inside, I cautiously moved around the rooms as if they were booby-trapped. Taking my time to peer around corners, stopping every few feet to listen for any kind of sounds, had started to try my patience. But I had no other choice. If I had any hope of escape, I had to be careful.

I wasn't afraid of Samuel, not in the least. The last time I'd lost a fight, I'd been in the fifth grade and it was only because there were three of them. I knew if I came up against the man who took Sara, he would be lucky to crawl out alive.

What I *was* afraid of was coming across him in one of the dark crevices of the house and strangling the life right out of him before I was able to locate Sara. I had to remind myself not to act without thinking, and to rein in my rage long enough to be able to rescue her.

Then all bets were off. Whatever happened...happened.

As I rounded the corner to enter a different room, I heard someone yell above me, followed by a loud crash. An object had been thrown against the wall, shattering into a million pieces.

If I was a betting man, I would guess Samuel had found the tracking device hidden in Sara's cell phone because the signal I had went dead at the exact moment of impact.

I heard heavy footsteps circling, the creaking of the floorboards above my head only adding to the direness of the situation. Samuel was probably pacing around, not quite sure if someone was on their way to rescue her or not.

But it was too late.

I was already there.

Before I took another step, someone wrapped their fingers around my arm, tugging me backward. Whirling around to fight off the intruder, I'd thankfully stopped my fist in mid air before connecting with the man's face.

It was Kael.

In my quest to save my woman, I'd completely forgotten he was following behind me for the past hour. He'd called me while I was enroute and offered to come with me. At first, I was hesitant, not wanting to endanger anyone else's life, but I quickly realized I could definitely use his help. With the two of us, we would surely be able to locate Sara quicker. Plus there was extra muscle in case we came face to face with her captor.

The sounds above us brought me back to reality. While Samuel was distracted by his own paranoia, we went to find Sara. We searched all of the rooms downstairs but to no avail. Obviously, we weren't going to check upstairs because he was up there, so we headed off to look for a basement door. I was living in my own horror film, so I prayed my reality mirrored the movies and she was down there somewhere. Once I located it, I twisted the handle slowly, the door creaking as it brushed across the floor.

Fuck. I hope he can't hear me. Not yet.

The only light we had to guide us was from my phone. Thankfully, it was bright enough for me to see in front of me, but not too bright to bring any unnecessary attention. We took the stairs slowly, unaware if there were any missing or rotten ones in our path. Once we'd safely reached the bottom, I made quick work of searching the darkened room.

All I saw were old broken pieces of furniture and piles of boxes, with God knew what in them, littering every corner of the room.

As we were about to head back upstairs and venture to the floor where Samuel was, I heard the faintest of sounds coming from somewhere nearby. I strained to hear, but the sound of my beating heart deafened me. Taking a couple of deep breaths, I was able to calm my anxiety enough to hear it again.

The sound flitted in the air all around me.

Where the hell is it coming from?

A faint whimper.

Heading off in the direction where I thought I heard the noise proved to be correct. As I came closer, the light whimpers turned into quiet sobs.

It was Sara.

She was crying.

Where the hell is she? My fingers glided over the rough wall, feeling for any kind of secret passage. Finally, I found a gap between the panels. When I pushed, it gave way to a door to another room.

Shining my small light through the darkness, my heart picked up pace as I saw a body lying on a bed not twenty feet in front of me.

I found her.

It took everything in me not to shout at the top of my lungs, but I had to be quiet. I needed as much time as possible to devise a plan.

As I walked closer, I noticed immediately her hands and feet were chained to the old, dirty bed. Rage instantly pumped me up, preparing me to rip him apart with my bare hands. My breaths, although controlled, were short and choppy, a pain radiating through my tightly coiled chest.

Calm down. You're no good to anyone if you can't focus on anything but your fury.

Talking to myself proved effective. For the time being, anyway. I took three more steps toward her, and although I was already teetering on the edge, it wasn't until I saw her eyes that I started to unravel.

Her gaze locked with mine but she looked straight through me.

As if I wasn't even there.

My heart broke.

~4~

Sara

Surely my eyes were playing tricks on me. I saw a man standing near me, but it wasn't Samuel. At least it didn't look like him. The small amount of light which shone from something in his hand wasn't enough for me to determine who was sharing the same space with me.

As he moved closer, the feel of the air changed. I sensed who it might have been, but I didn't allow my brain to go there.

The more he advanced, the more the energy bristled between us. Still, I didn't acknowledge who it could have been, there in the dark, musty old room, hidden in the basement of some crappy house.

Hope was the only thing I had left, and if he wasn't really there with me, then what was the point? I would beg for the cold hands of despair to strangle me. My mental status would have been zapped from me, hallucinations taking over and making me as insane as the man who took me.

"Sara. Can you hear me?" the man whispered, continuing to advance toward the bed, toward my chained-up body. His voice sounded like Alek's, but still I didn't give in to the dream of being rescued.

I closed my eyes and kept telling myself it wasn't real. None of it. I wasn't being kept chained in a smelly basement. I wasn't hoping and praying Samuel would kill me already and end it. I wasn't praying the man I loved would come and save me.

No...it's all a dream. I was going to wake up any minute, nestled into the crook of his arm, our bodies twisted around each other in his big, comfy bed.

"Baby," the voice called out again. Warm breath brushed my cheek.

Then a familiar scent invaded my senses. But could I be sure I wasn't simply fantasizing, the deepest recesses of my mind overpowering my sense of logic, of what was real or not?

Opening my eyes proved futile because I still couldn't make out anything except a looming form. Was it Samuel trying to trick me? *Don't say Alek's name. He might become upset and hurt you.*

I held my breath as fingers caressed my hair. I was trying to remain strong, but my walls broke. A tear escaped and dripped to the mattress below. Then another. And another.

"Don't cry, honey," he said. "I'm here now. I've come to take you home."

It *was* him.

Alek was really there to rescue me.

Before I could respond, I heard someone else descend the steps. Fear wrapped around me again. "Please," I begged. "Get me out of here." My body shook, the chains above my head making a loud rattling noise.

Reaching out, he stilled the clinking with his hands. "Don't move, Sara. We can't alert him. We can't risk it. Not yet."

Someone was moving closer to where we were. The door was pushed open and another light shone into the darkness. "Devera, did you find her?" *Kael?*

"She's over here. Help me find something to cut these chains."

"Chains?" Kael asked, more in astonishment than anything.

"I'll be right back, sweetheart," he promised before moving away from the bed to join his friend in the middle of the small room.

I knew better than to cry out, the fear ever-present Samuel would discover they'd come to rescue me. I remained quiet, my breathing slowed so I could listen for his footsteps. Alek and Kael moved about the room with the stealth of ninjas. I couldn't see too well, but my ears pricked to the slight noises they made. It was faint, but I heard the rustle of their shoes as they searched the room for something to break my binds.

Finally, I heard Kael whisper, "I think I found something that'll work." Both men rushed to my side. Something took hold of the large chains above me, and within seconds I heard a loud clanking sound.

It scared me.

It thrilled me.

Alek made quick work of freeing both my arms and legs. I'd been in the same position for what felt like forever, so when he tried to move me, I cried out. The blood rushed quickly to my limbs, the pain more than I thought it would be.

"Sorry, baby, but we have to get you up and moving. Breathe through it." He helped me to my feet and once I was steady, the pain in my hands and feet subsiding a little, I grabbed hold of his shoulders.

"I knew you would come for me." I became dizzy, the air in the room suddenly stifling. "You always come for me," I mumbled before I passed out.

The next thing I knew, I was being lowered to my feet. Awareness of my surroundings bombarded me like a heavy weight. "Are we still here?" I asked, my confusion slowly waning.

"Unfortunately, yes. We're on the main floor. We'll be out of here soon." Alek circled my waist and pulled me close, allowing me to rest against him for support.

Kael came up behind us, startling me and making me jump. "Sorry, Sara. Didn't mean to frighten you."

"Well, it's not hard to do." I tried to laugh, but there wasn't anything funny about what was going on around us.

"You ready?" Alek asked his friend, already moving in the direction of the back door.

"Yeah. Let's go," he answered.

As we stepped toward freedom, our movements were halted when Samuel walked directly in front of us. At first, he looked as if he was confused, glancing back and forth between the two men who had come to rescue me. Then his gaze fell on me.

He looked dejected, as if he couldn't believe I was leaving him.

Again.

He completely ignored Alek and Kael, his focus solely on me as he spoke. "Sara. Where are you going? Why are you leaving me?"

His voice was calm, posture rigid, his demeanor threatening.

Alek shielded me with his body, pushing me to step behind him. "Get out of our way, Samuel. We're leaving."

Kael added, "We've called the cops, so don't even try anything."

My captor completely ignored both of them, his attention still focused only on me. It was creepy, but had I expected anything less?

It was weird. I could deal with our situation when it was the two of us. Okay, maybe not *deal*, but at least no one else was involved. But having to watch Alek witness the bizarre back-and-forth between us was unnerving. I knew how much it affected him. His eyes were resolute as he stared at Samuel. Even through the dim lighting of the room, cast by a lamp in the corner, I caught a glimpse of his despair when I turned to look at him. An action my kidnapper didn't appreciate.

He took one step toward me.

Toward us.

"Don't look at him, Sara. Look at me," he demanded. "You belong with me. Not him. Why are you trying to run away? All I've ever done was love you." His words were slurring the more he spoke. Was he on something? Was he medicated at all? Because whatever it was didn't take the crazy out of him.

Alek reached down and gripped my hand in his, squeezing tight. His rage was breaching the surface; one wrong word and he would be in full-on attack mode. "Don't say another fucking word to her. Do you hear me?" he seethed, his muscles tensing in his anger.

Again, Samuel never acknowledged him.

Kael took a step to the side in an effort to make Samuel feel as if he was surrounded. Off in the far distance, I could hear sirens. *Hurry up.* I wanted to leave as quickly as possible, but I also wanted to make sure they caught him. His second time kidnapping me was surely enough for them to lock him away for the rest of his natural-born life.

He must have heard the sound of the police as well, because before anyone of us could even take our next breath, Samuel advanced, lifted his arm and pointed a gun at Alek.

I froze.

No. No. No.

This can't be happening.

As soon as he drew his weapon, Kael stepped closer and raised his own gun, pointing it directly at Samuel's head. Nerves racked through me, unaware of how everything was going to turn out. There were no guarantees. Scratch that. The only guarantee I could depend on was Samuel didn't care if he lived or died. He only wanted me. I could see it in his dead, blank stare.

"If you leave me, Sara, I'll kill him." He wasn't paying any attention to the gun Kael had aimed at him. It was almost as if he hadn't even seen it. Or him.

"Then you're going to have to kill me, because she *is* leaving and you're never going to see her again," Alek goaded. I tried to warn him with my grip not to antagonize Samuel. He ignored me.

"Samuel," I started. "Please, don't harm him. He has nothing to do with this."

"He does!" he shouted, his voice ringing out in the air around us. "If it wasn't for him, you would be with me. We would be so happy together." The tension in his voice became more strained as the situation unraveled.

I remained silent. I had no idea what to say to him. Uttering the wrong words would surely cause him to explode, and I couldn't take the chance. Not with Alek's life.

Taking a step forward so I was positioned directly next to Alek proved to be a fatal mistake. I saw the recognition in Samuel's eyes. He saw me as standing up for Alek, and it didn't sit well in his crazy mind.

His posture straightened.

He inhaled a deep breath, and I knew it was coming.

I couldn't see his finger on the trigger, but I sensed he was about to pull it.

So I did the only thing I could.

I jumped in front of the man I loved as the shot rang out.

As I was thrust to the side, then to the ground below, all I kept thinking was, *Is Alek okay? Is he hurt?*

I did my best to focus on the commotion around me but the more I stayed alert, the more the pain overtook me.

If I close my eyes, the pain will stop.

Slowly drifting off into the darkness, my only thoughts were of the man who always tried to save me. I prayed I was able to save him in return.

~5~

Alek

It all happened so fast. First, Samuel blocked our route to escape, then he was spouting off crazy shit about him and Sara being happy together and that it was all my fault. Like I'd gotten in the way. *Well, you're damn right I did. I put myself between the woman I love and a crazy-ass psycho.*

Everything after was a blur. For reasons unknown, Sara jumped in front of me to shield me from the bullet. I didn't even know how she realized he was going to fire it at me.

Didn't she know I would die for her?

Give my life to protect her?

Once the gun fired, I lunged forward without thinking and knocked Samuel back against the wall. I heard Kael shouting to me, but I blocked him out. The only mission I was on was to steal the life from him. I should have been checking on Sara. I had no idea how she was, but I chose to stay in denial a little while longer. Plus, I knew my friend would tend to her while I set about destroying Samuel.

Wrestling around on the ground proved to be more difficult for him than it was for me. I had rage and fear on my side, which allowed me to best him rather quickly. The first punch shattered his nose, the second knocked him out cold.

As soon as I stood, I ran over to check on Sara. Kael was kneeling over her body, shaking his head profusely as he tried to find the wound. There was so much blood, it was hard to locate exactly where the bullet had hit her. I prayed right then and there, asking God to spare her life and not take her from my world.

But my worst fears were coming true right in front of me.

Reaching down to check her over myself, my hands were immersed in her blood, the warm, sticky substance oozing from somewhere on or around her chest.

My fingers circled her wrist, trying my best to find a pulse. She had one, but it was weak.

"I've called 911, Alek. They'll be here any minute." The sirens we'd heard before were closer, maybe two or three minutes away. As I prepared to cradle Sara's head in my lap, I noticed movement in my peripheral vision. I turned toward the distraction and saw Samuel starting to come back around.

Sara laid there dying yet he had the audacity to breathe life? As if he was entitled to it?

I snapped.

Searching on the ground around me, I located his fallen gun, gripped it in my hand as if it was my best decision and moved toward the man who would forever change not only my life but Sara's, as well.

There was no way she was going to be the same after that night. He managed to rip away what little safety she'd felt after so many years living in fear.

As for me, he was going to be the first and only person whose life I would extinguish without a second thought.

I kicked his side when I finally stood next to him, the barrel of the gun pointed right between his eyes. Kael was still crouched next to Sara's body, holding her hand while he looked after me with concern.

"Alek, don't do it. Let the cops sort him out." I heard his words, but they meant nothing to me. They didn't even permeate my brain.

Ignoring my good friend, I placed all my focus on the man at my feet. He glanced up, and the look he gave me almost made me pity him. He was delusional and certifiable but in his head, he was normal.

"They'll see I'm better one day. They'll let me out, and I'll come back for her."

I never hesitated.

I pulled the trigger and watched the life drain from his eyes. Only when I was sure he took his last breath did I release the gun from my hand. It made the loudest noise as it crashed to the floor.

~~~~

I was going to wear a hole in the carpet if I didn't stop pacing, my impatience and nerves driving my legs to walk back and forth on their own accord.

I knew I was driving the hospital staff crazy with my incessant rants about wanting information on Sara. Every five minutes, I was demanding answers and each time, they told me I had to wait. Needing to hear something from the doctor was slowly eating me up.

I kept picturing Sara lying helpless on the floor, bleeding out right in front of me. All because she took it upon herself to try and protect me.

To save me instead of the other way around.

A wide range of emotions flooded through me. Anger and fear were battling for the title, and I wasn't quite sure which one was going to hold the belt in the end.

There were so many things I wanted to say to her. I only hoped I had the chance to tell her how much she truly meant to me. I also needed to express how angry I was with her. Upset she put her own life in jeopardy, a life I'd spent the greater part of a decade trying to protect. Without thought, she tossed it all away, threw caution to the wind with one fateful, selfless and stupid decision.

The more I thought about what had transpired, the more my chest hurt. *If I don't watch it, I'm going to be lying right next to her. We could be roommates.*

In the middle of my internal meltdown, I noticed two people walking toward me in the waiting room. Looking up, I saw Alexa was holding on to Matt's arm, despair written all over her face. I'd filled them both in when I went to look for her, so when I placed the call she was in the hospital, they knew it wasn't good.

Matt helped Alexa to her seat before he approached me. He really wasn't a bad guy. Actually, the more I saw him interact with both Sara and Alexa, the more comfortable I was with him being in my woman's life. He cared for them as if he was their brother. I had to admire that.

He extended his hand and, for once, I took it without reservation. He was almost as worried about his dear friend as I was.

"How is she? Have you heard anything? What happened?" he spouted, question after question falling from his lips without a break.

"I don't know how she is," I grated. "These bastards won't tell me a damn thing. All I know is she was taken into surgery four hours ago."

"Surgery?" Alexa cried. "What happened, Alek?" She held my gaze until her face dropped into her hands, sobs racking her body as she wept for her best friend.

"She was shot." Three of the worst words I'd ever muttered in my entire life. "Honestly, I don't know anything yet. The doctor hasn't even been out to update me on her status. Hell, I don't even know if she's still in surgery."

Matt stared at me as if he held me responsible for Sara's predicament. Could I blame him? I would forever carry around the guilt until my dying day.

Without saying a word, Matt joined Alexa on the small sofa in the corner of the waiting room. We glanced at each other from time to time but other than those fleeting moments, we sat and waited in silence. Well, *they* sat. I continued to do what I did best: pace.

When I thought I couldn't take it anymore, a doctor came strolling into the room. *Where the hell is his sense of urgency? Doesn't he know the love of my life lay clinging to life somewhere in this hospital?*

"Mr. Devera?" he asked as he looked around the room, trying to pinpoint which one of us was going to answer. When I walked closer, basically announcing I was the man he was looking for, he opened his mouth. *Please, tell me good news.*

"Miss Hawthorne's surgery went well. Luckily, there wasn't too much damage to her shoulder. She should have full range of motion after some physical therapy. Other than that, she'll be fine."

Her shoulder? I could have sworn she was shot directly in the chest. I was preparing myself to receive news the bullet had pierced her heart.

Because that was exactly what it had done to mine.

"When can I see her?" I asked, standing a little too close to him.

"I'll send a nurse out soon to take you back. But please, don't stay too long because she's still quite woozy from the anesthesia. Plus, she

~ 35 ~

needs her rest." He left before I could ask him any more questions. His staff had probably warned him about me, so he made sure to give me an update then got the hell out of there.

Sure enough, not five minutes later, a nurse escorted us back to Sara's room.

"Normally, we only allow one visitor but seeing as how you all have been here for hours, we'll make an exception this time. Don't be too long because she needs her rest."

I quickly thanked her before rushing to Sara's beside.

My heart all but stopped when I saw her lying in the bed, looking damaged and broken.

My soul broke apart inside me, piercing my heart like tiny razor blades, making me bleed out all of my hurt, anger and fear.

~6~

Sara

I was lost between delirium and reality when I saw him approach. He looked so broken, like a piece of him died when he rescued me. With each step he took, I could see the immense love laced in his eyes, but there was also a great fear lurking underneath.

Knowing he must have been going out of his mind with worry the whole time he was unable to find me, I wanted nothing more than to comfort him. I had no doubt he was beating himself up, taking the blame for my abduction.

He was crazy protective over me, and the realm of his sanity had surely been tested.

"Hi, beautiful."

I croaked out a response, my throat too raw and painful to provide anything more than a garble. Pain bombarded me with a fierceness I'd never felt before; it almost took my breath away. I winced and cringed from the slightest movement. My arm hurt but since the pain radiated all over, I wasn't quite sure where the actual damage was. I also wasn't in any shape to comprehend even if Alek explained it to me.

Curiosity won out, though. "What happened? I remember Samuel standing in front of us as we were trying to leave, but my memory is a little fuzzy after that." I flinched one more time, my arm slipping off the propped-up pillows.

"First things first," Alek interrupted. "Do you need a nurse?"

"I think so. My arm is killing me."

"I'll call someone in, Sara," Alexa said. It wasn't until I heard her voice did I even take notice there were other people in the room with us.

Both Matt and Alexa were patiently standing behind Alek, waiting for their turn to visit with me.

How did I not see them standing there?

"Thanks, Lex," I mumbled, my speech slurring as I spoke.

Fixing my eyes back on Alek, I asked him again about what happened. I knew something was off because although I was still in pain, my comprehension, speech and movements were slowed, no doubt from the effects of whatever drugs were pumping through my body.

"He tried to stop us as we were all leaving. Then you...you..." He trailed off, the end of his sentence too much for him to recall.

"Who else was there?"

"Kael. You don't remember him being with us?"

Memories flooded back the more he spoke. I vaguely remembered his friend being in the house. My brain was still a little hazy, but I think I recalled him holding my hand as I was lying on the floor.

Bleeding.

Fading in and out of consciousness.

"Sara? Are you okay?"

"What?" I asked, still having difficulty focusing. "Yeah, I'm fine. It's taking me a little while to remember. That's all."

"Why don't we discuss this a little later? After you've had time to recuperate more?" I could tell *he* was the one who didn't want to talk about what happened. Before I had the chance to answer, Alexa came back into the room, a nurse following behind her.

"Look who I found! And it looks like she has the good shit with her, too." She winked, trying her best to lighten the mood. When she rounded the bed and stood beside me, she reached down and clasped my hand. The look on her face was sad although she was smiling. She was doing her best to make me forget, even if for a moment, and I couldn't be luckier she was my best friend.

I knew they were all scared. Shit, *I* was scared and I'd been the one to live through it. Twice.

When Alek saw the nurse was attending to my pain, he physically relaxed. Whatever the wonderful woman had put in my IV, it was taking effect and fast. My eyelids became heavy, the pain in my arm dwindling to a mere throb. I was suddenly tired, and although I wanted to visit a while longer, I knew my body had a different plan.

Alexa squeezed my hand before giving me a quick hug. "I'll come back tomorrow, Sara. You need to rest. Love you."

"Love you, too," I grumbled, the drugs kicking in full-force.

Giving both men a hug, she made her way toward the door. Before she could disappear, Alek called out to her.

"Alexa, wait. I'll walk you out." He was such a gentleman. I knew Matt would have walked her out, but I could tell he wanted to spend more time with me. "I'm running to the cafeteria on my way back up," he mentioned, turning his attention fully on Matt. "Do you want anything?"

To say I was shocked would be an understatement. Even in my hazy state, the mere fact he was so pleasant with my friend was astounding. I'd seen subtle changes over the past couple of months when it came to dealing with Matt, but to witness it in such an obvious way threw me for a loop.

"Nah. I'm good. Thanks, though." Matt nodded and turned his attention back on me as Alek and Alexa exited my hospital room.

"When did you guys become best buds?" I whispered, falling into a coughing fit because my throat was so damn dry. Matt instantly poured me a small glass of water, stepping closer to my bed and holding it to my lips so I could drink.

"Are you all right?" he questioned. I hated I was the one who caused him to worry about me. All of them. At the same time, though, I was beyond grateful I was surrounded by such wonderful people.

After my throat had been soothed with cool liquid, I was able to speak a little better. More coherently. "I'll be fine. Stop worrying about me, Matt. I can see the look on your face." I reached for his hand. The moment we touched, his eyes became glassy, fear for me suddenly overwhelming.

"I was so scared something bad happened to you, Sara." He shook his head, gripping my hand tighter. "I mean...more than that psycho snatching you up. When I got the call you'd been found but were rushed to the hospital, I immediately thought the worst."

I tried my best to comfort him. I found it funny I was the one lying in the hospital bed, my shoulder all mangled to hell, yet I felt bad for making everyone else worry about me.

The more the minutes passed, the sleepier I became until I could no longer keep my eyes open. Matt had stopped talking, knowing I wasn't paying attention any longer. I hoped he wasn't offended, praying he realized my body wasn't my own any longer.

The last sight I saw before my lids closed was Alek strolling back into the room, his attention solely on me as I drifted off into a healing sleep.

~7~

Alek

I knew damn well once Sara woke up and was lucid enough she was going to want to know what happened. The full story. Doing my best to prepare myself for when the time came, I squared my shoulders and paced the room.

She'd been asleep for six hours. I saw her stir at one point, her face contorting in a bad dream. I prayed she wasn't reliving the very real nightmare she'd recently endured. I couldn't protect her in her dreams, and it killed me.

"Alek," she called out, causing me to instantly rush to her side.

"I'm here. How are you feeling?" I reached for her hand and the instant we touched, I was calm. Constantly being on edge was starting to wear on me. I knew I had to take it easy, but it was hard to convince myself to do so. Reminding myself Sara was alive and would fully recover should have been enough for me to relax. But it wasn't.

An odd thought crept in, one I'd had before when I was on my way to save her from Samuel. A feeling I pushed to the back of my mind, not having enough emotional energy to deal with it in the moment.

She was safer before you barged into her life.

Pushing everything aside, I focused all my attention back on Sara.

"My shoulder is killing me but otherwise, I'm okay."

Trying to dislodge my hand from hers, I offered, "I'll call the nurse so she can give you something for the pain."

She held tight, her strength surprising me. "No. I'll deal with it. While the meds dull the pain, I can't focus and all I do is drift off to sleep." She squeezed my fingers. "I want to talk to you about what happened. My mind is still a little fuzzy."

I averted my eyes, not wanting to have to relive what she'd gone through. Hell, what *I'd* gone through.

"Alek. Please, tell me what happened. Help me remember so I can move on." My lips parted and I inhaled a deep breath but before any words slipped out, Sara's breathing changed and she started shaking.

At first, I thought she was having some kind of reaction, her body convulsing in warning. But the closer I looked, I saw the fear in her eyes, and it had nothing to do with what was going on with her physically.

She was remembering something, and it was freaking her out.

"Where is he?" Where is Samuel?" She closed her eyes and waited for me to respond. I took some time before answering, trying to figure out the best way to tell her what I'd done. "What? Where is he? Oh, my God, did he escape?" Her eyes remained closed as she fired off question after question at me.

Stroking her hair in an effort to try and comfort her, I leaned in close and hovered above her.

"He's dead." She remained silent, for countless seconds. "Did you hear me, Sara? Samuel's dead. He'll never harm you again, baby."

Still nothing. Her chest was barely moving and for a second, I thought she'd fallen back asleep, right in the middle of her paranoia.

"How?" she asked, her eyes finally opening and focusing on my face.

I didn't hesitate. I had no regrets about taking his life. None whatsoever. I'd do it again in a heartbeat if it meant she would be safe.

"I killed him."

The gasp which fell from her lips broke my heart. She seemed conflicted, not sure what she should feel. She had to be relieved he was no longer a threat, but I think she was also concerned for me, for what I'd done.

Tears instantly streamed down her face, followed quickly by uncontrollable sobs.

Running my fingers over her cheeks and trying to catch her tears, I tried my best to soothe her. "Please, don't cry, Sara. It's over. It's done." My voice was as calm as I could manage, and I think my composed tone was what finally settled her.

"Talk to me, baby. Why are you crying? You're safe now. He will never threaten you again."

She finally spoke, a breath of relief rushing out of me.

"I'm relieved he's no longer here, Alek, but the fact you were the one to end his life is what I'm upset about." I was going to interject, but she instructed me to let her finish with a simple glance. "I never wanted you to be the one who would have to live with the regret of taking his life. It should have been me. I should have put a stop to this...to him." Her look was pitiful and I almost chastised her, demanding she stop blaming herself and allow me to carry the burden. "I'm so sorry," she whispered.

"Stop it right now. I don't ever want you to be upset about what I did. I chose to end him, Sara, and I would do it again in a heartbeat, over and over if I had to. He threatened your life for the last time. I did what had to be done. Plus, I couldn't live with myself if you'd been the one to pull the trigger, because I would never want *you* to bear that burden."

Our eyes locked. It was as good a time as any to fill in whatever blanks she had about what happened. So I dove right in, telling her all the horrible details, making sure to express how upset I was with her for putting her life in danger, to which she simply smiled and stroked my cheek. When she questioned how Samuel had even found her, I hung my head in regret. He was able to locate her whereabouts because of my carelessness. I'd been selfish. I'd been the one to drag her out to the charity event. At the time, Samuel had been securely locked up but I still should have known better. I hadn't given it a second thought when the paparazzi snapped photos of the two of us. Not protecting her identity had been one of my biggest mistakes.

A little while later, after all questions had been answered, she decided she needed the pain meds after all. It didn't take long before she was drifting off into what I hoped was a peaceful sleep.

~8~

Sara

My stay in the hospital lasted for a total of eight days. Initially, I was healing rather well but on the fourth day, I developed a pretty nasty infection in my wound. Luckily, it was able to be flushed with a heavy concoction of antibiotics, taking until day six to feel somewhat normal again.

Thankfully, I was given the all-clear to go home two days later and boy, was I ready.

I was so sick of lying in that uncomfortable bed. I was tired of people having to go out of their way to come see me, the only purpose being to check in and see how I was coping. Alek stayed with me the entire time, only leaving to attend meetings he simply couldn't cancel. I argued with him to go home and rest, but he wasn't listening to me. He would placate my demands with a simple nod. Then when I fell asleep, he pulled the cot the nurse had brought in for him close to my bed, holding my hand until he drifted off.

Alexa and Matt had come by many times to say hello and check on me. I appreciated their concern, but I wanted everyone to stop fussing already. I was going to be fine. I'd survived worse.

Or was that the worst of it?

The weeks after my hospital stay were a blur, my time eaten up with physical therapy appointments four times a week. The thing which frustrated me the most was there didn't seem to be an end in sight.

Trent, the therapist assigned to me, informed me it could take up to six months before my arm was back to normal. He was optimistic I would have full range of motion, but only if I was faithful in keeping up with all of my set appointments. Otherwise, I could suffer slight immobility. There was no way I was going to let that happen, though. Wanting all traces of what had happened to be gone, I grunted through each session.

But no amount of therapy would erase the scars which were left behind.

Both physical and emotional.

Alek was extremely tolerant the entire time, which I really appreciated because there were times when I wasn't the best patient. He drove me to and from my appointments, insisting he stay the entire hour.

I knew some of his reason was due to the fact my therapist was a man, who was also easy on the eyes. Alek's whole body would tense up when Trent had to touch me, but it was his job. He had to ensure I was properly stretching and completing all of the rotation exercises.

Each time his hand made contact with my shoulder, or any other part of my anatomy, I would glance over at Alek and watch as his chest expanded, his hands balling into tight fists as he stared at us. Once he caught my eye, he would give me a tight smile, silently telling me he was working on his jealousy issues.

One time, when he thought Trent was too touchy, he approached him and threatened physical violence. I apologized and had to take Alek into the back of the room to chastise him.

"You have to stop this. Now. He's not being inappropriate with me at all and you standing there, brooding the whole time, is not helping me. And it's not helping Trent do his job properly. Don't you want me to get better?" I was beyond irritated with him, with my recovery...with everything.

"Of course I do!" he hollered, his own frustrations barreling off him.

"Then stop acting like a jealous teenager," I chastised.

"Then tell him to stop groping you." He stood his ground and waited for me to back down. Well, it wasn't going to happen.

"If you don't knock it off, Alek, you're going to have to leave." When my threat did nothing to dissuade him, I decided to try a different approach. Moving closer, I placed my hand on his cheek. He leaned into my touch and for a brief moment, I thought he was going to loosen up. But he remained as stoic as ever. "I'm not attracted to

Trent, not in the least. All I'm thinking about the whole time he's working on me is how I'll be able to throw my arms around you and hold you tight." Dropping my hand from his face, I took a step back. "But if that's not something you would like, then please, keep acting like a jealous fool."

He showed his surrender to the situation by simply nodding, giving me a quick kiss and retreating to lean against the wall. He shoved his hands deep into his pockets but I could tell he was still clenching his fists, the fabric of his pants bulging with every action.

Alek was acting exactly how I knew he would. It didn't excuse his behavior, but I understood where his head was at. I knew how I would have felt if the situation was reversed and a beautiful woman had her hands all over him, even if she was acting in a professional manner.

Yeah, I would much rather be on this side of the fence.

~9~

Alek

Sara was recovering quite nicely, although her impatience increased with each passing day. I had to remind her the process was going to take time, but there were days when she didn't want to hear any of it. So I backed off and gave her my unwavering support.

Frustration was certainly a new emotion for my woman. Well, when I wasn't the cause for it, at least. When she couldn't lift something or extend her arm to grab an object from a shelf, she would grunt, grimacing in aggravation. I tried my best to remind her pushing herself too fast wasn't a smart choice. Some days, she would listen to me and others, well, she ignored me as if I hadn't said anything at all.

She couldn't stand relying on others for help, especially at work, a place where she was really hindered. I never thought I would be so thankful she had Matt there to help her. He'd really stepped up as her friend, and as an employee. He constantly went above and beyond for her, opening up the shop in the early morning hours as well as closing up late whenever she deemed she'd had enough for the day.

After witnessing more interactions between the two of them, I realized the way he looked at Sara was exactly how I'd looked at my sister Mia. A brother to a sister, full of love and adoration, and my favorite emotion of all...protectiveness.

While Sara was struggling with her physical limitations, I was doing my best to go back to the way things were before she was taken from me, but I found it difficult. Samuel's death was not the issue. While there was an innate feeling deep inside me at the memory of taking another man's life, it wasn't guilt or remorse. I thanked God every day I woke up and that bastard wasn't alive. Never having to worry about her safety where he was concerned was a huge relief. I think the emotion which crept up now and again was...surprise. I'd obviously never been the cause for someone else taking their last breath. But whenever the odd sensation arose, I remembered the crazed look in his eyes as he mumbled, '*They'll see I'm better one day. They'll let me out and I'll come back for her.*' Once the memory rushed forward, I pushed everything aside and focused on Sara and her recovery.

The real issue which plagued me was ever since I stepped foot into her shop on that beautiful, fateful day, I'd inadvertently put her in danger.

Before she met me, she was safe. I'd made sure she was protected all those years. But since the day I'd made the selfish decision to force my way into her life, she'd had one encounter after another, thankfully none of them fatal.

I knew I had a decision to make, and the thought it was going to ultimately crush us both, ending life as we knew it, made my soul weep at the inevitable.

~~~~

"Hey, hey. What's the good word, my man?" Kael sang out as soon as I uttered my greeting into the phone.

"Not too much," I replied, forever thankful my good friend had moved back to Seattle. I'd known Kael since we were young boys. We were inseparable most of our lives, but his job took him to California years before, the only communication between us being a phone call every so often. Luckily, our time apart had been short-lived.

I didn't normally talk about my feelings, except with Sara, but I knew I needed to bounce some things off Kael. He was the perfect sounding board because I knew he wouldn't judge me. He might give me advice I didn't want to hear, or tell me when I was being an ass, but he would listen and hear me out.

"What time did you want to meet up tonight?" I asked, counting down the hours until I could gain someone else's perspective on my issue. I'd already informed Sara I was going out for a couple of drinks after work. At first, she was only too happy to hear I'd made plans. Admittedly, I was slightly offended she wanted to get rid of me so quickly, but after she explained her reasoning, I wasn't so pissy. She hated I'd been fawning all over her for the past few weeks, never taking a night for myself. So when she'd heard I was going to be spending some much needed time with Kael, she was thrilled.

"Whatever time you can pry yourself away from work is good for me," he answered.

"Okay, how about I meet you at seven? At Billson's?"

"I can pick you up if you want and we can go together," he offered, a slight twinge of humor to his voice.

"This isn't a fucking date." He laughed at my outburst. "I'll meet you there."

"Yeah, I guess you're right. Plus, you're not my type," he joked before hanging up the phone.

Still smiling, I dialed Sara's number. I'd bought her a new phone due to her other one being destroyed. Soon after she'd become lucid in the hospital, she asked me how I'd ever found her and I had to tell the truth. It was because of the tracker I'd put in her phone after I learned of Samuel's release. She never argued with me, a small smile appearing on her lovely face before she drifted off to sleep. This time around, I made sure to ask her if it was all right if a device was installed on her new phone. Without hesitation she agreed; the added comfort of me being able to find her if she ever needed me was what made her comply.

"Hi, honey," she answered on the second ring. I could tell from the rushed tone of her voice she was busy but wanted to at least talk for a few minutes. It drove me nuts when she didn't answer her phone and instead of us arguing over it, she did a great job of placating me. I would have thought after eliminating the one real threat in her life I would have calmed down, but if anything I became even more protective. I couldn't understand it myself, so trying to explain it to Sara was near impossible.

"Hey, babe. How's your day going?"

"Good. Busy, but good. I really need to hire someone to help out around here. Matt and I are struggling these days. We have a couple of part-timers to help with deliveries, but it's not enough." Blowing out a frustrated breath, she continued with, "Thankfully, business is booming, but we're a little stressed. Plus, not having the full use of my arm yet is hampering me even more." I heard her call out to Matt about an order before she came back on the phone. "Sorry, Alek, but I can't talk now. Can I give you a call later on?"

"Sure thing. But remember I'm meeting up with Kael for a couple of drinks, so how about I swing by your place afterwards?"

"Sounds great to me. And Alek?"

"Yeah."

"Please have fun. You worry too much."

"I'll try. For you, I'll try."

After our conversation ended, I saved and closed the two spreadsheets I had open, grabbed my keys and headed out to meet Kael.

Arriving before him, I grabbed a private booth far from the rest of the patrons. Billson's was a really nice, casual yet elegant establishment. It had private sitting areas, as well as high-back tables and chairs. I'd been there before for business meetings and really enjoyed the food, the service always being on point. Plus, the atmosphere was calming, which was a plus since I was a bit on edge.

Lost in my own head, I almost missed Kael as he entered. I waved him over once I caught his attention.

"Have you been here long?" he asked as he took his seat at the other end of the small couch, throwing his keys on the table. Before I could give him an answer, he cut me off. "Sorry I'm late, but Adara and I sort of had a fight before, so..." He trailed off, obviously not wanting to finish his statement.

"Is everything okay? Is it serious?"

"It'll be fine. And yes, I think it's serious, but she doesn't. But then again, what's new, right?" He looked around for a waitress, anxious to place his order. Thankfully, he didn't have to wait long.

Once the waitress was close enough to see us, she blanched. We knew the sort of reaction we obtained from women when we were by ourselves, but when we were together, it was almost too much. We knew we were blessed with good looks, but we never flaunted it. Well, not since the day our women had stolen our hearts, anyway.

After she'd composed herself enough to take our order, she left us alone to talk.

Needing more time to figure out what I wanted to say to him about my issue, I asked, "Do you want to talk about it?" I knew what it was like to have my woman twist me up so badly I didn't know which way was up. He definitely had my sympathy.

"Thanks, but no thanks. I don't want to think about it anymore tonight. All I want to do is drink and hang out."

"Sounds good to me."

It took two hours after we'd arrived before I was comfortable enough to bring up what was plaguing me, the multiple bourbons aiding the situation.

"So..." I started, indicating there was something important I wanted to talk about. And it worked, turning Kael's attention on me.

"What's up?"

"Well, you know everything that went down with Sara recently."

"Yeah..." he answered, his curiosity piqued.

"I've been feeling a certain way about it. About her. I mean, I love her and everything; that hasn't changed. Actually, I love her more each day, but I just...I don't know." I didn't know the best way to verbalize whatever it was I was thinking.

I was confused, plain and simple.

"If you love her, then what's the problem? Is it because you ended up killing Samuel? Because you could speak to someone to try and work through it."

"No, that's not it at all." My face scrunched in instant aggravation. I hated the mere sound of his name.

"Then what is, because you're losing me here, man." He was certainly confused. I was rambling, not really focusing on any one point.

The waitress came over asking if we wanted refills. I admittedly answered yes while Kael declined. I hadn't started off wanting to drown my sorrows in alcohol, but it was where the night was leading. I knew I was going to need to call my car service soon. There was no way I was going to drive to Sara's intoxicated. She would kill me. If she ever drove drunk, or even tipsy, I would be so angry with her I would never let her forget it.

Against my protests, Sara had stopped living with me after she came home from the hospital. She said she didn't want to rush anything, arguing our relationship was still being tested and she didn't want to jeopardize the progress we'd made so far. I knew the imminent threat was abolished so I didn't really have a leg to stand on. I gave in, for the time being.

"I don't really know. Well, I kind of know, sort of." I took another sip of my drink, letting the ice cubes crash to the bottom of the glass before putting it back on the table. Finding Kael's confused expression, I continued on in my senseless ramble. "You know I've been watching Sara for close to a decade now, always trying to keep her safe. Well, it seems like ever since I barged into her life, up close and personal, I've been failing to protect her. Things have happened to her which wouldn't have had I kept to the original plan, which was me off in the shadows, shielding her from afar."

"You can't really believe that. She's the best thing to ever happen to you, and you to her. I see how you two look at each other when you're together. It's as if no one else exists. I know, because it's exactly what I have with Adara. It's a rare thing to find in this fucked-up world, Alek." He knit his brows before he spoke again. "Don't tell me you're planning on breaking it off with her, because you think you're doing more harm than good being in her life. Because it would be the stupidest thing you could ever do."

He knew exactly where I was going with my conversation and because of it, I couldn't even look him in the eye. I knew he would try and talk me out of it, telling me I was an idiot if I went through with what I was contemplating.

I loved Sara more than I could ever explain in words, but the thought of her being taken from this world because I was unable to protect her was unbearable. I was too close. Her love, her very being, was distracting me from my ultimate goal, which was ensuring she was as safe as could be, each and every minute of the day. I knew it was a lot to put on someone, but it was a weight I was only too happy to carry.

Honestly, I didn't know what I was going to do. The thought of not being able to see her, to touch her whenever I needed to feel her against me, or to even hear her voice was torture. But I knew I had to make a decision either way because what I was tormenting myself with, over and over, was driving me to drink. Literally.

Before we left, Kael gave me his parting words of wisdom. "Listen, Alek, I know you love her and she loves you. I think you're letting what happened cloud your judgment. You need to take a step back and think everything through before you make a rash, stupid mistake. Please, tell me you'll think about it before you make any decisions." I stared at him, trying my best to compute his words. The last drink really did me in. My brain was fuzzy, and the words which spilled from his mouth sounded jumbled together. Kael broke the silence with his persistence. "Promise me, Alek."

"Fine, I promise I won't do nuthin' rush till I speak about it." *What did I just say?*

"All right, buddy, come on. You've had enough. We need to get you home."

As soon as I stood, the world spun around me. Normally, I could handle my alcohol, but it'd been a long time since I'd consumed so much. Thankfully, I'd called the car service a half-hour before, so my ride was already waiting for my drunk ass.

After paying our tab, we headed outside. Each step I took was staggered, Kael doing his best to hold me upright. The cool evening air helped my inebriated state, but only for a minute. My driver held the door for me as I stumbled inside, but before he locked me in, I yelled out to Kael, who was standing only a few feet away. "Hey, do you need a ride?" I slurred.

He chuckled and shook his head. I knew the state I was in was going to be enough for him to hold over my head for years to come. Not since we were in our early twenties had I drank to such an excess.

"No. Unlike you, I haven't had much to drink, so I'll be fine to get home on my own."

"Okay, dress yourself then."

"Don't you mean suit yourself? Boy, you're really gone aren't you? Do you need me to hold your hand and put you to bed?" he teased.

"Fuck you." I laughed, giving him the finger as I situated myself in the backseat of the town car.

Once I made eye contact with the driver, I spouted out Sara's address and settled in for the ride.

I hope I don't pass out.

~10~

Sara

A loud crash in my living room woke me from a sound sleep. I instantly shot up in bed, clutching the covers under my chin as if the material was going to protect me somehow.

I strained to hear something, anything, but it was quiet. A few seconds into my paranoia, I heard someone walking down the hallway, running their hands along the sides of the walls as they approached my bedroom door.

The handle jiggled before the door crashed open.

There in the hallway stood a tall figure and at first I was terrified, until I realized it was Alek. Reaching for the bedside lamp, I flicked it on, illuminating the room enough to see his looming form.

He didn't move, just stood there staring at me. His hair was disheveled, as were the clothes he wore. The black tie around his neck was lopsided, his white dress shirt sloppily hanging over his suit pants. He looked a mess, yet still completely sexy.

It wasn't until he was near the bed did I notice he was swaying, barely exerting enough energy to remain on his feet. When I glanced up into his face, my breath rested in my throat. The look in his eyes was daunting. Hopelessness had taken over, and I wasn't quite sure why.

We were doing so well lately, all things considered, and I didn't want anything to upset our delicate balance. Sure, he still had his demanding ways but I was used to dealing with him, so whatever tiffs arose were quickly resolved. All I wanted to do was move forward with our lives.

I'd planned to have a conversation with him over the next few days about moving back in with him. Officially and for good. He had been asking me more frequently as of late and I'd refuted him each time, not wanting to upset the progress we'd been able to make in our relationship. Many things had happened during the short time we'd known each other but thankfully, we'd been able to forge ahead.

My decision to live with him made sense. If I wanted our relationship to move forward, it would be the next logical step. Plus, I hated traveling back and forth between my place and his. I wanted one location we could both call home.

There was something else I'd been holding back, as well. Three words. I tried to tell him I loved him once before but he'd been sleeping. I wanted him to hear my words, to see the affection for him shining in my eyes as I spoke those words to him. I wasn't holding back any longer, especially glancing at the look of despair etched into his face. I wanted to rid him of whatever was bothering him, and I knew my words would do it. Professing my love for him while he was drunk wasn't ideal, but I didn't want to shut myself off any longer. Although, if I'd thought about it, the first time he told me he loved me was not perfect, either. The important thing was we *did* love each other and those feelings should never be stifled, no matter what was happening around us.

Alek moved closer until his knees hit the bed, reaching down so he could touch my face. "I love you, Sara. I always will, no matter what." The last few words were slurred, but I heard him clearly enough. He sounded conflicted about something, and it was obviously bothering him. Anguish and heartache were evident in his beautiful green eyes, even as he professed his love to me.

I reached out and tried to pull him next to me but he remained standing, which was a feat considering he looked like he'd drank himself into oblivion.

His next words rang out into the silence of the room, confusing me even more. "I need to protect you, but I can't...not this close to you."

My heart skipped a beat. "What are you talking about, Alek? Why are you being so weird right now?" He was starting to freak me out but instead of delving into whatever he meant with his words, I decided to ignore it, against my better judgement, and switch the subject. "Why don't you let me help you undress, then we can go to bed," I offered. Looking into his gorgeous face, I silently pleaded with him to comply.

Letting out a breathy sigh, he replied, "Okay."

I moved to the edge of the bed and helped him remove his suit jacket. He kicked off his shoes and socks as I unbuttoned his shirt. My fingertips grazed his skin as I pushed the expensive fabric off his shoulders. He stood in front of me and waited for me to remove his pants. Slipping his belt through the loops, I yanked it free and tossed it to the floor. The clink of the buckle rang out across the room, the only other sounds coming from our anticipating breaths. My hand grazed over his erection as I slipped the pants down his muscular thighs. Before I could free him from his boxer briefs, he whipped them off so fast I was surprised he didn't fall over in his haste to toss them aside.

Running my hands all over his chest, I parted my lips and leaned forward. I wanted to kiss and suck his sinewy skin, but before I made contact, he gripped my arms and pulled me into him, crashing his chest against mine.

"I want to make love to you, Sara. I want to cherish and remember this."

Again I chose to ignore his statement, instead moving my face close to his. "I don't think you're in any state to do such a thing right now." Truth be told, I was shocked he was able to become hard. I'd never seen Alek intoxicated before, but I had assumed men couldn't perform if they had too much to drink. Alexa had complained about it before with previous sexual conquests. But I should have known Alek would defy the typical circumstance.

"I'm as hard as a rock. All I need is your sweet pussy to take me home." His mouth claimed me, nipping and tasting as if he hadn't kissed me in weeks. He turned and flopped on his back, laughing as he took me with him. My fingers weaved through his thick hair, holding him in place as I returned his relentless passion. Breaking the kiss briefly to inch up the bed, he pulled me along with him, moving me so I was straddling his lap. I had nothing but a flimsy pair of panties covering me, a tiny camisole shielding my chest from his eyes. His hands moved from my waist, up my body and searched for my breasts. When he'd made contact, he pinched my nipples, teasing and tormenting me until they pebbled under his touch.

"Do you want me to take this off?" I asked as I bit my lip in expectation.

"Uh-huh," he mumbled. His eyes were glassy but he was fully in the moment, never taking his gaze from my face. His tongue snuck out to wet his lower lip. The sight spurred me further, lowering myself so I could taste him. While he smelled like liquor, my need for him pushed me forward until our tongues danced together, dueling and vying for dominance over the other.

He was winning.

Coming up for air, I quickly pulled the cami over my head and tossed it to the side. Before I could remove my last piece of clothing, he moved his hands back to my hips and ripped the material from my body with one swift motion.

"Oops. So sorry," he garbled. His grin gave him away, trying to be playful and in control all at the same time.

"I'm not." I tried to make a joke, but there was nothing funny about the need pulsating between us. I wanted him to bury his beautiful self so deep inside me, it would be impossible for one of us to move without the other.

Before I could plead for him to take me, he raised me up and placed me so I was hovering over the tip of his cock. "Aren't you forgetting something?" I asked, a look of confusion playing on his face.

It took him some time but it finally registered he needed to put on a condom. My need to connect with him wouldn't deter us from being safe.

"Oh, yeah." I half-expected him to roll his eyes or make a comment, trying to convince me otherwise, but he didn't.

As soon as the protection was rolled all the way on, he entered me in one quick thrust, causing both of us to cry out. I thought in his current state he was going to take me hard and fast, but instead he stayed true to his word.

He made love to me.

Slow and sensual.

"Come here, baby." He pulled me close to his mouth so he could savor me. "I love you so much." His lips were gentle against my own, his teeth coming out to play every so often, nipping my swollen lip. He was driving me crazy; so much so I tried to increase the pace but he would slow down even more.

I found my perfect opportunity to express exactly how I felt about the man who was deliciously driving me crazy. Placing my hands on his chest, I slowed our movements until I made him stop. The look on my face caused him to tip his head to the side in confusion.

"I love you, Alek. I'm so sorry I haven't told you before now. I tried to tell you once, but you had fallen asleep. Then...the next day..." I couldn't finish my sentence. I didn't want anything from the past to taint the tender moment happening between us right then.

He remained silent, staring at me as if I was a stranger. He looked perplexed, as if he was battling a war inside his head. "Alek? Are you all right?" *Maybe it's the alcohol jumbling his brain.*

A few of the longest seconds passed before he answered me. "You love me?" he asked, a sexy smile tipping up the corners of his gorgeous lips.

"Of course I do. I've loved you for some time."

"Not as long as I've loved you." He groaned before pulling me in for another heart-stopping kiss.

My body rocked on top of his, the gentle friction against my clit driving me insane. There was definitely something to taking it slow. His hands reached further down my body and gripped my ass, driving himself in deeper, pulling me even closer. He rained kisses along my jaw, moving to nip his favorite spot below my ear before making his way back to consume my mouth.

My breathing changed, my heart ramming against my chest as my fingers dug into the thick of his hair. The sweetest pressure built inside me and I chased the feeling like I'd never done before. He knew I was on the precipice of exploding soon, so in one fluid movement he flipped me on my back, thrusting into me with a need he'd been holding back until right then. Gone was the sweet and slow, but I wasn't complaining. I loved when Alek couldn't contain his passion for me, taking me hard and fast until he pushed me toward the edge of bliss.

"Alek," I panted. "I'm so close. Are you almost there? I want you...to come...with me. Please." I buried my face in his neck, letting his essence invade my nose, intoxicating me with his masculine scent.

"Yes...but I don't want this to end. Ever. I love being inside you. I can't function without it." His hips plunged forward, increasing his pace as he chased his orgasm. "Tell me you love me again. I need to hear you tell me," he demanded as he punished my body with his need.

"I love you, baby. I love you so much." Our mouths crashed together, our breath mingling, muffling our cries as we both fell over the cliff.

I would never get enough of his exquisite touch. He knew exactly what to do to make my body come alive. And the way he was able to affect my emotions was incredible, the good *and* the bad. In reality, he was the answer to every prayer I'd ever had, and I knew my heart would never be mine again.

It belonged only to him.

Forever.

After we came back down from our high, he moved so he was cradling me from behind, his fingers caressing the soft skin of my belly.

We fell asleep wrapped in each other's arms.

The next morning, I woke up to an empty bed and an uneasy feeling wrapped around my heart. He said some pretty strange things the night before, and I prayed his words were solely a result of the alcohol he'd consumed.

Don't become paranoid now, Sara. Not after everything you've been through together.

The next couple of days Alek seemed distant, evasive even. When I asked him if there was anything wrong, he would placate my concern by telling me he was stressing about a building issue with a new hotel.

I believed him.

~11~

Alek

I continued to struggle with the dreaded emotion which seemed to snatch my very sanity. Everything swirling around inside me barely made sense. I knew in order to keep her completely safe I would have to take a step back, but of course, I was finding the feat extremely difficult.

How could I walk away from the only woman I'd ever loved?

How could I breathe if she wasn't in my life?

But something had to give. And I feared it was going to be my heart.

I tried to keep as busy as possible, slowly distancing myself from her, first physically then emotionally. I quickly learned both were nearly impossible. I had to keep drudging on, though, if I was going to ensure nothing bad would ever happen to her again.

I was grateful for every single moment Sara bestowed on me, putting up with my ranting and mostly unreasonable demands. She didn't understand the protective need I had over her. She would never fully understand, I suppose, no matter how many times I tried to explain it to her.

My promise to her grandmother so many years before started off innocent enough but it turned into something deeper. It turned into my need to save her from the dangers lurking behind every corner, to save her from herself.

I knew Samuel was her biggest threat and he'd been extinguished, but the tragic situation only drove home how unfocused I'd really become those past few months.

I knew I sounded paranoid, but it was the way it had to be if I was going to protect Sara once and for all.

~12~

Sara

"What's happening, chickie?" Alexa asked as she came bouncing through the front door. Braden walked closely in right behind her, as if he didn't want to let her out of his sight.

"Hey, you guys. How are you?" I smiled, but I wasn't in a happy mood. I was putting on a front these days, mainly because I didn't entirely know what the problem was.

"Hi, Sara," Braden greeted. He followed Alexa into her bedroom only to be escorted out five minutes later. He looked hurt but appeasing. "Bye, Sara," he said before he dragged my dear friend into the hallway, away from my curious eyes.

I was so happy Lex had found a good man. They've been spending more time with each other and I was happy she had someone to turn to, especially since my accident. I knew she worried about me, and I was glad she had a shoulder to lean on in times of need.

She came back ten minutes later, a look of pure happiness etched across her face. She couldn't help but look the part of a woman in love, although she said she wasn't there yet. I thought she was lying to herself, holding on to the remaining hardened part of her fragile heart.

Alexa Bearnheart acted tough, but she was a huge softie underneath.

"Why did Braden leave? I could've gone into my room if you guys wanted to hang out here and watch TV." I scooted over on the couch to make room for her to sit.

"Don't be silly, Sara. I told him to leave." Grabbing a pillow, she sat down and pulled it close to her, getting comfortable for what I was sure was going to be one of our talks.

"And why would you do that?"

"Because I saw your face as soon as I walked in. You looked like you were going to burst out crying but were trying your hardest to look *normal.*" Reaching over to grab my hand, she gave it a squeeze and said, "I know when my girl is struggling."

I half-smiled, trying to keep my tears at bay. I didn't know what was wrong with me lately.

My shoulder was healing well.

The shop was doing great.

My nightmares were fading each night.

The only thing left was Alek.

In all of the time we'd been together, I'd only questioned his feelings for me once, and it was when I discovered he'd been watching me for close to a decade. Otherwise, I knew he cared for me, loved me even. He'd said so on numerous occasions, and they weren't just words; his actions proved as much, as well. But after he rescued me, I felt him slipping away, and I didn't know if I was being paranoid or if something was really going on with him.

"I need a glass of wine," I mumbled, unfolding my legs from underneath me as I rose from the couch. "Do you want some?"

"Do you really even need to ask?" She laughed and threw the pillow at me, hitting me in the back of the leg as I walked toward the kitchen. "So, spill it, Sara. What's going on with you?"

"Can you wait until I have a drink before I answer?" I was trying to joke, hoping some forced humor would do something for me, but it didn't. Not at all. What I really wanted to do was take the entire bottle of wine, climb under my covers and lose myself in oblivion.

I walked back toward the couch, bottle of wine and two glasses in hand. Kicking the pillow up with my foot, I flung it across the small space, actually hitting Alexa in the face with it.

Now *that* made me laugh.

"Well played, Sara. Well played." She laughed, as well.

She took the glasses from me and poured the drinks, sitting back in silence and waiting for me to start talking.

She arched a brow and I spoke. "Oh, Lex, I don't know. I don't know what's wrong with me. Actually, I do but I'm so confused."

"Does it have something to do with Alek? Did you guys have a fight?"

"I wish it was so simple, because then at least I would know where I stood. No, it's something else entirely. I think he's distancing himself. He's different when we're together now, which, by the way, is becoming less and less frequent."

"Well, didn't you say he was stressed out over a new building issue? Maybe it's why he's not been around as much. It's possible that's all it is, Sara."

"You don't see it. You don't feel it like I do. Like the other night, for example, when he came here drunk. He was rambling on about how he would always love me no matter what, and he needs to protect me but can't do it when he's so close to me. It was weird. He was *not* acting like himself, drunk or not." For as much as I tried to hold back, I failed. A lone tear escaped and ran down my cheek. I wiped it away quickly, not wanting any more of them to fall and halt my conversation with my best friend.

"Is he the reason we're now down one table lamp?" she teased.

"Yeah, sorry. He must have bumped into it when he came in. I'll pick up another one."

"Don't worry about it. I think you have enough on your plate." She finished her glass and poured another.

"Thirsty, are we?" I asked as she took a few sips of the cool liquid.

"No, simply trying to squash my raging hormones." She took another sip, swallowed and said, "He practically attacked me in the hallway, whispering all sorts of dirty things in my ear before letting me go. Then he simply saunters down the hallway like nothing happened."

I didn't want to be the reason she wasn't spending time with her man. "You can call him back, Lex, seriously. I don't mind at all."

"I wouldn't even think about it. You need me more than I need to have sex." She tipped her head to the side as if she was contemplating the two. "Yeah, you need me more," she repeated. "End of story. I need more wine, that's all." She laughed. We sat in comfortable silence. That was the great thing about having a friend like Alexa. We can just be. We can sit together and not speak, all while still supporting each other.

Finally, I broke the silence. "Maybe he's having a tougher time with killing Samuel than he even realizes." Simply saying those words made me shudder. "I can't even imagine being responsible for taking another person's life, no matter what the circumstances. The guilt I have for putting him in that situation will always be there, but he must be dealing with something unimaginable."

"Have you tried to talk to him about it?"

"Yeah, but all he does is shut down. He won't talk to me, or anyone else." After some contemplation, I nodded slowly. "Maybe that's what the issue is." I figured if I said it aloud I could make it true, although the uneasy feeling never wavered.

"I bet it is, Sara," she said comfortingly. Poor Lex. She looked as hopeful as I was. She truly was a great friend.

"When was the last time you saw him, or even spoke to him?"

"The last time I saw him was when he came by drunk. But the last time I spoke to him was this morning. He's been busy all day in meetings and hasn't had much time to talk."

I missed him.

I missed talking to him on the phone.

I missed his arms wrapped around me, holding me tight.

I missed his lips on mine.

I even missed arguing with him.

After another hour of talking, we decided to call it a night. The fact the bottle of wine was empty probably had a little something to do with our persistent yawning. At least I felt better having had the chance to talk to someone about what was weighing on my mind.

~13~

Sara

"Hey, watch yourself," Matt called out as he came up behind me. He was carrying a breathtaking bouquet of white and burgundy calla lilies, and my distractedness almost made him drop them all over the floor.

"Wow, Matt, did you put the arrangement together yourself?"

"Sure did." He leaned in close and revealed, "I learn from the best."

"Well then, you must be talking about Katherine because she taught me everything I know."

"Yeah, she's who I was talking about." He laughed, making his way back toward the prep room.

"Very funny," I yelled over my shoulder.

Inventory kept me busy. There were only a few customers milling around the store, and I was thankful for the short reprieve to catch up on some basic data entry.

The bell above the door sounded as someone walked in, pulling my attention from the computer. A young, blonde woman made her way toward me, a bright smile lighting up her pretty face.

"How can I help you?" I asked in my usual upbeat, professional tone. Even if I was in a bad mood, or distracted by something not so pleasant, it all changed as soon as I was dealing with my customers. They were my lifeline, after all.

"Hi. Yes, I wanted to know if you were hiring."

Her inquiry came at the most unusual time. Matt and I were discussing the other day how it would be nice to have another pair of hands with the day-to-day orders and deliveries. But I didn't even have the chance to place an ad or put up a simple 'Help Wanted' sign in the window yet.

"Well, I was contemplating bringing in an additional person to help out, but it would only be part-time. Is a part-time position something you would be interested in?" Truth was, I was still learning the business part of the shop and according to my financials, I couldn't really afford to bring someone on full-time. Not yet, at least.

"Part-time would be perfect." There was something about the woman standing in front of me I couldn't put my finger on. She seemed friendly enough but she regaled me with real interest, as if she thought she knew me from somewhere. Then again, it could've simply been nerves. Maybe I was paying too much attention to something which was a figment of my imagination.

Looking the girl over from head to toe one more time, I dove right in with the necessary questions. "Do you have any experience working in a flower shop?" I quickly assessed my potential employee, doing my best to read her during the whole two minutes she'd been in my shop. She looked to be older than me, maybe in her early to mid-thirties, but in this day and age, I couldn't really be sure. Her personality seemed pleasant, and she had an air of confidence surrounding her.

No outward signs of crazy.

Then again, there was only so much you could tell from an initial interview.

She smiled brightly as she answered. "I do have experience, close to ten years' worth. I used to work in my aunt's shop back home in North Carolina."

I didn't need much time to make my decision before I blurted out my proposal. "I'll tell you what. I can bring you in on a trial basis. Let's say a month. We'll see how you fit in and what your skills are before a permanent offer is extended." Her smile widened which caused me to mirror her enthusiasm. "What do you say?"

"Oh, my God, that would be amazing. Thank you so much."

"Okay, great. Well, you can come by tomorrow, say around ten?" As we were finishing up, Matt strolled in with a different array of flowers in his hands.

Grabbing his attention, I introduced him to our newest addition. "Matt, this is..." I stopped talking because I realized I'd never gotten the poor woman's name. "I apologize, but you never told me your name."

"Oh, yeah, it would be helpful, right?" She gave Matt a once over, obvious attraction in her stare. "It's Megan. Megan Smith."

"Hi, Megan." Matt looked over at me, a look of confusion clouding his face.

"I decided to hire Megan on part-time, on a temporary basis. If she works out then we'll have a new member on our team."

"Oh, cool. Nice to meet you," he said before making himself scarce again.

Having no idea where my head was at, I thought it important enough to tell her my name, as well. "My name is Sara, by the way. You might need to know it." We chuckled together but her real focus wasn't on me; she continued staring at Matt as he walked away. I didn't blame her, but she'd learn soon enough she didn't have a shot with him.

Oh, well. Who am I to ruin the poor girl's fantasy?

When her eyes returned to mine, she blushed quickly then said her goodbyes as she walked out the door. I really hoped Megan worked out because we could definitely use the help. There were three other part-time workers, but I had to cut back their hours because two of them were in school and needed to focus on their studies and the other woman was set to have surgery on her elbow.

Walking around the counter to grab another pen, I heard my phone ding, indicating I'd received a text message. Opening it, I saw it was from Alek.

> *I won't be able to see you tonight. Too many things to straighten out with a deal to get away. Alek*

Figures.

Sadly, his message didn't surprise me, which was disheartening. I was too disappointed and paranoid over our tender relationship to even text him back. I needed some time to think, or over-think, as Alexa would say, about whatever was going on recently between us. I knew he had other pressures on his time, but he never let it hamper us from being together before. Normally, he would simply re-arrange his schedule in order for us to see each other.

So, what was different?

Distractedly, I muddled through the rest of my day. My thoughts kept floating back to Alek, to the man who had quickly become my heart...my everything. I knew we'd experienced something devastating in our short relationship, but it was merely a test, right? A trial of our love for each other. Something which would bring us even closer.

I thought Alek and I could battle any weather, but our storm was proving to be too much, threatening to tear the roof off our lives.

I texted him twice after I arrived home from work but he never answered. I was hurt, wallowing in my own crazy thoughts when I decided to call it a night and go to bed. It was still early, but I longed for the sweet arms of sleep to drag me under and not release me until a new day had arrived.

~14~

Alek

The text I sent to Sara was utter bullshit, but I didn't know what else to do. Of course I had pressing work issues, and of course I was having a hell of a time with getting my new hotel up and running, but shit like that never stopped me from seeing her before. Nothing stood in the way of us spending time together.

Without even asking, I knew my odd behavior was weighing on her. I knew I was an asshole for putting her through it, especially after she'd finally revealed her deepest feelings for me.

When she uttered the three words I'd been longing to hear, a piece of my soul broke away. I knew she meant every word, and for as much as I held those words tight, I knew nothing would ever be the same between us going forward. So, I cherished our night together, then, like a coward, slipped away in the morning before she even woke.

I was still a man conflicted. Loving Sara made me feel alive, made me whole. But her life was more important. Her safety, to be exact. I knew exactly what I had to do, even though it would tear me up inside.

Staying away from her was going to be my ultimate challenge, but I had to do it. Otherwise, I ran the risk of endangering her forever simply because of the hold she had on me.

My phone's shrill ring busted into my thoughts like a sledgehammer.

"Devera," I answered curtly. "What? Are you fucking kidding me? Well, why did he go back on his initial quote? Goddamn it! All right, I'll be there in the morning." I ended the call, even more irritated than before. The new deal was taking so long to lock down, causing so many unforeseen complications.

One more thing to add to my plate.

The only good thing to come out of this debacle was I would be away for a few days trying to work everything out with the developer. Which meant I wouldn't be tempted to do or say anything rash, something I might regret later on.

Since I'd been acting like such a dick lately, the least I could do was stop by to see her the following day before I left town.

It was close to noon when I walked through the front door of Full Bloom. I was met by a stranger manning the front counter.

Who the hell is she?

The woman instantly made eye contact, but the look she gave me mirrored my own.

Truth be told, I wasn't used to such a reaction from women, so looking at the annoyance written all over her face threw me.

Actually, the way she looked at me was as if I'd killed her dog.

"Where's Sara?" I asked, still doing my best to figure out who she was.

Realizing she should appear to be somewhat professional, she plastered on a fake smile before answering me. "Is there anything I can help you with, sir." The *Sir* tumbled from her lips as if it was poison.

Before I came back with a retort, Sara walked into the front of the store, her head thrown over her shoulder as she yelled something back at Matt about an order.

When she turned her head in my direction, she stopped dead in her tracks. Looking at me as if she'd seen a ghost, she grabbed onto the edge of the counter top to steady herself.

What the hell is wrong with her?

"Alek? What are you doing here?"

I walked closer and reached for her hand. "Can I talk to you? Outside?"

I didn't even give her a chance to respond before I pulled her out the door and away from the woman shooting daggers my way. Ushering her toward the back seat of my town car, I opened the door. Without reservation, she stepped inside, scooting across the seat to give me some room.

The air instantly changed. I hadn't realized how much I missed Sara until she was two feet away from me. The skirt she was wearing rode up on her thigh when she tried to situate herself on the smooth leather of the seat. My eyes were immediately drawn to her supple skin, remembering her on top of me as she rode me the last time we were together.

"What did you want to talk to me about?" she asked, pulling the hem of her skirt lower. Her breathing quickened when she noticed me ogling her, but she tried to seem unaffected.

I thought she'd be all smiles and hugs and kisses when she saw me but weirdly, she looked annoyed to see me. I couldn't blame her, really. I'd basically pulled a disappearing act on her over the past week.

My lips parted to answer her question, but she cut me off before I could say a word. "Oh, and thanks for basically causing a scene back there, too."

"What are you talking about? I didn't cause any scene."

What the hell is she talking about?

"You dragged me out of there like you were pissed. Anyone can tell by looking at you that you're annoyed and itching for a fight. So what? What's the big problem this time?" *Oh, great.* I wasn't with her two minutes before she started in on me.

Well, let's go, sweetheart.

I should have allowed her the time to settle down and not fueled her bad mood because I knew I was the cause for it. It was all my fault, so I should've kept my mouth shut. But I didn't. Of course.

Instead of delving into the fact I was going away on business, I chose another topic altogether.

"Who's the woman?"

"What woman?" she asked, irritation laced around each word.

"The strange woman working the counter in your shop." My eyes flashed anger and my body tensed as the seconds ticked by. But I kept my temper in check, knowing damn well Sara didn't deserve any of it.

"She's my new employee. Her name is Megan and I hired her on part-time, on a temporary basis. If it's any of your business," she chided.

I leaned a little closer to her. She was hiding something from me but then again, wasn't I keeping my own secret? The more we sat in silence, the more it looked as if she wanted to smack me. But there was something besides anger looming behind her gorgeous eyes. The faint appearance of fear and sadness were hiding in there, as well.

I fought against every instinct I had to reach out and pull her to me, to ravage her mouth and claim her. Exhaling a deep breath, I leaned back against the seat and decided the best course of action right then would be to find out all I could on the mystery woman.

"What do you know about this woman? Where did she come from? Did you do any background checks on her?" I rattled off questions faster than she could answer me.

"Of course, I did some checking on her. I called all her references and they all gave her high recommendations." For a split-second, she looked like she was going to tell me something else but decided not to at the last minute.

"I want her social security number, Sara. I'm going to run my own background check on her."

"No, the hell you're not. I got this, Alek. I'm taking care of it."

"Well, why didn't you at least tell me you hired someone?"

"When was I going to do that? During all of our lengthy phone conversations? Or maybe I could have told you when we actually spent some time together." Yeah, she looked like she wanted to hit me right about then. She shifted her body and moved closer. "Wait," she said as she raised her finger in the air. "None of those scenarios happened because you've been avoiding me like the plague."

I immediately broke eye contact and looked out the window. Yes, she was upset with me, but it went much deeper. I was being a coward because I didn't want to see that look, the look which told me I was chipping away at her heart little by little.

"Well, you still should have told me somehow," I spit out, still glancing at the people walking by.

"Fuck you," she whispered, drawing my attention to her immediately. Sara had only told me to go fuck myself one other time. I deserved her anger, but her words hurt just as much as the first time.

Her voice choked up and I saw her try and catch her breath. Before I could react, she raised her hand and wiped away a lone tear.

My heart broke.

I wanted to comfort her and explain everything but it didn't fully make a whole hell of a lot of sense to me, so I remained silent. After some time had passed, she spoke again in a much calmer tone. "Why did you come here today? It wasn't about Megan, because you didn't even know about her until you walked in."

"Yeah, I know." I couldn't keep the sarcasm from my retort. Our encounter was not what I'd envisioned. As I sat next to her, the last thing I wanted to tell her was that I was going away for work. It may have gone over smoother had we not gotten into an argument, but now it was going to add to the ever-growing tension bouncing back and forth between us. "I have to go away for a few days, Sara. I have to deal—" She cut me off before I even finished speaking.

"With some business issue, yeah, I know. Same old excuse." She gripped the handle as she prepared to leave. With her back turned toward me, she asked, "Is there anything else?"

Before she was able to escape, I reached for her wrist and halted her movements.

"Sara, look at me," I demanded. She didn't comply at first but when I tried to tug her into me, she turned her head in my direction. I knew if I pulled her into my arms, the tears which were gathering behind her saddened eyes would spill over, causing both of us to break. I never wanted to hurt her. Ever. But apparently it was exactly what I was doing.

"I love you." I uttered the words, hoping to bring some sort of solace to the both of us, but it had the reverse effect. Another lone tear broke free and slid down her flushed cheek.

She pulled free from my grip, opened the door then slammed it shut, rattling not only the window but my very soul.

~15~

Sara

Hurrying back inside, I was so distracted with my interaction with Alek I almost ran right into Megan. Thankfully, she maneuvered out of my way quick enough so neither one of us was knocked on our ass.

The look on my face must have been enough to silence her from asking me anything. I mumbled an apology and rushed past her to the back room.

"Whoa," Matt warned as I almost barreled into him. *Two for two so far.*

"Sorry. I... need a minute." I pushed my way into the small break room and plopped down in one of the chairs. Thankfully, Matt saw the look on my face and left me alone with my wandering thoughts.

Unfortunately, Megan was too new to give me the same consideration.

She came around the corner and poked her head in to see how I was doing. "Are you okay, Sara? Is there anything I can do for you?"

I smiled as pleasantly as I could and tried my best to mask my annoyance at being bothered. Internally, I chastised myself. She was only trying to be nice; plus, I would have done the same thing in her shoes. "No," was my simple and short answer.

"Who was that guy? He didn't seem very nice."

Apparently, she's not done.

I was shocked to see she wore an expression of dislike for the great Alek Devera. Women never reacted to him in such a way. I wished they did, but normally they were falling all over themselves, vying for his attention. Maybe she wasn't attracted to men. Before the thought fully formed, I quickly dismissed it, simply from her reaction when I introduced her to Matt. She pretty much undressed him with her eyes as she watched him walk away. I wasn't saying I wanted my new employee going after Alek...I simply found her reaction to him surprising.

"He's my boyfriend." I found my words sounded odd to me. Technically, Alek *was* my boyfriend, but it didn't really feel like it as of late.

Megan's response was a quick bellow of air and a roll of her eyes. Obviously, she wasn't a fan. Well, neither was I right then, but I wasn't about to air my dirty laundry. Especially to a virtual stranger.

When she continued to linger in the doorway, I had no choice but to ask her to leave. "Megan, can you please give me a minute to collect my thoughts?"

"Oh, sorry. Sure thing, Sara. Let me know if you need anything, okay?" I nodded in response as she turned around and walked away.

An hour had ticked by when I'd decided not to spend any more time wallowing in self-pity. I grabbed my phone and dialed Alexa's number.

"Hellooooo," she answered playfully.

"Hey, are you free tonight? Because I really need to go out and let off some steam."

"You must be in some sort of mood if you want to go balls-out, Sara."

"I am," I huffed. "I really need a distraction tonight, and the only thing I can think of is alcohol, maybe some dancing and my best friend. What do you say?"

"I say count my ass in." She mumbled something to someone before returning to our conversation. "What time did you want to go?"

"I'd like to start as early as possible. I'll meet you at home then we can get ready and go."

"Sounds great. See you later."

"Bye." I hung up the phone and let out a much needed sigh. I really needed the escape to take my mind off Alek and our relationship, or lack of one recently.

~16~

Sara

We started off our night with a couple of glasses of wine at home. I was a bit tipsy by the time the cab showed up, which should have been a sign to head back inside and go to bed. Refusing to listen to my nagging inner voice, I sat back and enjoyed the ride. Against my protests, Alexa had convinced me to go to Throttle. I didn't want to be reminded of Alek but I gave in, knowing my friend loved the place. Hell, so did I—minus the fact he owned it.

Once we'd arrived at the club, we lucked out grabbing the last two available seats at the bar. I wasted no time ordering a drink. We sat there for what seemed like forever, waving off unwanted advances from some brazen men. My thoughts were unfortunately consumed with one man; no matter how hard I tried to push him out of my head, his image was persistent. Much like the man himself.

"Does Braden know we're out?" I teased, knowing Alexa had her own stubborn guy to deal with. At least I wasn't alone there. Although I would've given anything for Alek to actually act like he cared about where I was or who I was with. Something. Some kind of recognition to let me know he still cared about me. About us.

"Yeah, he does." A quick look of annoyance danced across her face, but it disappeared before I could question it.

"Does he care?"

"About what? The fact I'm out?"

Swaying a bit, I gripped onto the edge of the bar. "Yeah. Does he give you a hard time when you go out?" I took a quick sip of my drink, relishing in the numbness snaking through my entire body. I never waited for her to respond, just continued to babble on. "Alek gives me a hard time whenever I go out without him. Not because he doesn't want me to have fun or he doesn't trust me, but because he can't smother and watch over me every minute. Well, he *used* to give me a hard time," I declared, taking another sip from my glass. "I don't think he gives a shit anymore." My eyes welled up, but I pushed back the emotion.

I need another drink.

"I wish there was something I could do or say which would help you, Sara." She ordered us another round, swiveling around on her stool to survey the other patrons.

The house music was pumping and people were drinking, letting loose and having a great time. I wanted to be one of those people, but my mind wouldn't fully release me. More alcohol was the answer, I was sure of it.

"Lex, I have to use the ladies room. Be right back."

"Okay, but hurry up because the band will be coming on soon."

I nodded and walked toward the bathroom, taking it slow because my feet weren't as cooperative as they were an hour before. Thankfully, the line wasn't too long. While I was waiting, I decided to check my phone. I didn't know why. It wasn't as if Alek had made a habit of calling me a lot recently.

So when I saw I'd received a text from him, I was utterly shocked.

Sorry about today, Sara.

That's it? After the way he'd been acting, he should have apologized for much more. How about, *I'm sorry I've been an asshole lately?* or *Please forgive me for basically ignoring you since you professed your love for me?*

Feeling bold, I decided to text him back.

Don't worry, Alek. I've already forgotten all about it. In fact, I'm going to drown myself in alcohol and have the best night of my life.

I hit 'send', stepped inside into an open stall and handled my business. When I was washing my hands, my phone chimed. I wasn't surprised he responded so quickly. I purposely texted him what I did hoping for a reaction. But I wasn't lying. I really *was* trying to drown myself in some liquid numbness. I'd pay for it the next day but right then, I didn't care.

Not funny, Sara. Where are you?

I'm so *not going to tell him where I'm at.* Although, all it would take would be one phone call and he would surely find out.

Moving back toward Alexa, I hopped on my barstool and for the first time that evening, I had a smile on my face. Okay, maybe it wasn't a smile, but it was definitely a smirk. I'd been able to catch his attention and I was going to do, or *not* do, whatever necessary to keep it. *Lord knows it'll be fleeting.*

As I took a sip from my fresh drink, my phone alerted me to another text.

Woman! If I have to track you down, I will. Then I'll drag you out of wherever you are and lock you up in my house. Forever, if that's what it takes. Tell me where you are. Now!

Where was all of this last week, or even the last couple of days? He'd been acting so distant, but as soon as I went out without his supervision, he wanted to act all demanding and controlling? *To hell with that.*

I'm where I'm at, Alek. You won't find me, so don't bother looking. Besides, I would hate for you to waste any unnecessary energy or thought on little ol' me.

I turned off my phone after I sent my last text. I didn't want to go back and forth with him all night because it would sour my mood even more. Plus, he was ruining the nice buzz I had going on. All I wanted was one night to forget. One night to let go and be free from all of the emotional turmoil which was my current life.

Alexa saw me typing away then shut my phone off. "Everything okay?"

"Yeah. Fine." I leaned over the bar and waved to the bartender. I placed yet another drink order, sat back down and stared at my phone. I didn't know what I thought would happen. It was turned off, for God's sake.

Alexa knew right then what my intentions were. We'd gone from a fun night out to her being worried about me. "Sara, don't you think maybe you should slow down a bit? You've had a lot to drink already, and I really don't want to hold your hair back while you puke it back up later." She smiled, but I knew she was serious.

"I'm not done yet, Lex. I need one more drink to push me over to being completely numb," I mumbled, clinking the ice cubes around at the bottom of my empty glass.

Thirty seconds later, the bartender placed our drinks on the bar and asked, "Which one of you is Sara?" He was holding a phone against his shirt to block out some of the noise.

How the hell does he know my name? Alexa pointed toward me and smiled, knowing damn well who was on the other end of the phone.

"Mr. Devera wishes to speak to you," he said as he pushed the phone at me. "You can take it in the back office, down the corridor to your right."

Scowling at him, I yanked it from his hand as I approached the office. Not surprisingly, the door was unlocked.

"Hello," I teased in my sweetest voice. Big mistake. The sounds which came from the other end of the receiver were almost indiscernible. I had to hold the phone from my ear because he was yelling so loudly. When he finally took a breath, I interjected. "What seems to be the problem, sweetheart?" My smirk was back, giddy I was able to rile him up.

"Don't play games with me, Sara. Now, go find Alexa and get your ass home where you belong."

What the hell? How did he know I was with Alexa? How long was he talking to the traitor of a bartender before he got me on the phone? *Mr. Turncoat must have described my friend to him.*

"Why don't you come down here and make me?" I would normally never instigate him in such a way, knowing full well he would actually come down there, cause a scene, throw me over his shoulder and stalk out of the club. But it was exactly why I did it. The uncertainty of our relationship actually had me craving his caveman tendencies.

"Sara...don't." He exhaled into the phone. "I can't. I just can't."

"Why, Alek? What the hell is going on with you? With us?" I was full-on drunk, letting go of any and all inhibitions and saying whatever came to mind.

"I'm not going to talk about this right now. Just get Alexa and go home. Now." His temper was controlled. I knew he was feeling guilty over something, but he wouldn't say what and it was driving me crazy.

I stomped my foot like an errant child and pushed back against his crazy demand. "I'm not ready to go yet, so I'm not leaving. But when I *do* decide to go, on my *own* terms, maybe I'll find someone to give me a lift. You know, someone who's actually looking to give me some attention."

Taunting him was not the right move to make. Even though we were physically separated, I was still waving a red flag in front of an aggressive, pissed-off bull of a man.

The next sounds I heard were a barrage of obscenities, then something crashing in the background.

Then the phone went dead.

My heart was beating so fast inside my chest. It was the most interaction I'd had with Alek in days, and of course, it was not a favorable one. He tried to tell me what to do, acting as if he even cared, and I pissed him off with basically telling him I might go home with some random stranger.

Way to go, Sara.

As I headed back toward the bar, I saw Alexa's full attention was on the band which started playing five minutes prior. She was even singing along to the song, a bright smile plastered on her face. Until she saw me approach. Then her whole demeanor changed. She slid off the barstool, grabbed our stuff and reached for my hand. "Come on, Sara. Let's go."

"What? No, I'm not going anywhere."

"Alek wants me to take you home, and I think he's right. You've had too much to drink, and I don't want anything to get out of hand."

My eyes narrowed in confusion. "How do you know he wants you to take me home?" She broke eye contact and fumbled with her keys, glancing at her phone before looking back up at me. *Oh, for God's sake. He texted or called her and had a little chat. And she fell for it.*

I didn't even need for her to confirm it. I knew exactly what happened, and for the first time that evening I wasn't going to fight it. I was suddenly drained. All I wanted to do was curl up in bed and wait for a new day.

I snatched my things from her hands and stalked toward the front door. Or should I say stumbled toward the front door.

We were in the back of a cab two minutes later. Resting my head against the seat, I caught movement in my peripheral vision. Alexa was texting someone, and I knew it wasn't Braden. Taking a chance, I blurted out, "Tell him I said to go to hell," before turning to look out the window.

She didn't say anything in response as we drove toward home.

~17~

Alek

Holy fuck, she is infuriating! I had half a mind to go over to her place, throw her over my knee and give her the spanking she deserved. I was losing my patience. I was trying my best, trying to be the man she needed me to be, but I was struggling.

My phone chimed with a message from Alexa, letting me know they were in a cab and on their way home. After what Sara had insinuated, I lost it, but instead of saying something I would later regret, I simply hung up on her. Then I texted her friend. Thankfully, she was in agreement, ushering Sara from the club immediately. I was grateful she had someone close to her to look out for when I couldn't be there.

The more thought I gave it, the more I knew I had to engage the services of my good friend, Calvin. He was the one person I trusted over the years to watch over Sara whenever I couldn't. He owned his own P.I. firm and he was the best at what he did. It wasn't much of a challenge watching her before because she lived a pretty sheltered life, especially after what had happened.

It was even easier now because she was walking around with a tracking device in her phone, one she agreed to have. Thankfully, she carried it everywhere with her. It was how I found her at Throttle, even though it wasn't a hard guess, seeing as how I knew both of them loved the place. From her responses, she was either too drunk to figure out how I'd tracked her or she'd simply forgotten it was on her phone. Either way, I wasn't reminding her.

Thankfully, Calvin answered on the second ring.

"Alek. How the hell are you? It's been a while since I've heard from you. Everything all right?"

Calvin Herdsman was based in California. He'd done a lot of traveling for me over the years, but luckily he wouldn't have far to go with the new assignment.

"Depends on what you mean by 'all right'." I allowed a brief moment of silence to linger between us before speaking again. "I need your help again, friend. The woman, Sara Hawthorne, the one you were helping me out with before? Well, I need you to look out for her for a few days while I'm away on business."

"Whatever you want, man. You know I'll be there to help you. Does she still live at the same address?" I heard him shuffling through some papers, no doubt trying to find the file he kept on her.

There was another pause before I answered. "No, she up and moved to Seattle about a year ago."

"She did?" he asked, sounding confused.

"Yeah. I've been able to keep an eye on her, but I have to go away for business and would feel better knowing you had my back while I'm gone." I didn't want to divulge all the details of our recent relationship. The only thing I wanted to hear from him was that he would drop everything to help me out. I knew it was short notice, but I'd pay him whatever he wanted if it meant her safety and my peace of mind. I wasn't so crazy this time around because Samuel was no longer a threat, but to be safe I wanted an extra pair of eyes on her.

"Okay, yeah, sure. When do you want me to be there?"

"Tomorrow."

"Tomorrow? Damn, Devera, nothing like giving me some notice." He blew out a breath of air before continuing. "Okay, let me move some stuff around and I'll be there in the morning."

"Great. I'll send you all the details."

"Sure thing. Talk to you later."

A wave of relief washed over me after we'd hung up. I needed to start making the transition back to the way I handled things before.

Before I'd made the best and worst decision of my life.

Before, for my own selfish reasons, I walked into her shop and drew her into my world.

I texted Sara to let her know I was leaving early the next day and would be away for a week. I'd initially thought it would only be three days but more issues arose with the new building plans. I also informed her I would be back late Friday and would see her then.

She didn't text me back. I wasn't surprised.

~ ~ ~ ~

It'd been four days since I last had any communication with Sara, and it was weighing heavier on me than I thought it would. But I couldn't break. I had to be strong.

Calvin provided me with daily updates. So far, everything was fine; nothing out of the ordinary. He reported back she retired to her residence after she closed up the shop, never leaving her apartment once she was home.

I knew she was hurting, and the thought alone was almost enough to make me pick up the phone and give in, to tell her I was an asshole and beg for her forgiveness. When those moments crept up on me, I instantly grabbed a drink, downing it to abate my momentary weakness.

My phone alerted me to a text as I was preparing to take a shower. I'd assumed it was work-related, so I was surprised it was actually from Sara.

We need to talk when you come home –S

I was dreading our talk because it would mean the end of us. The more time which passed without communication was more time for it not to be real. But once we talked, once we ended our relationship, it would cut me. Deep.

> ***Ok***

My response was curt. I knew Sara was dealing with this all by herself, going about it blindly because I refused to let her know what I was thinking. But I couldn't tell her because all she would say was that I was being ridiculous and somehow, she would talk me out of it. Then I would be back to square one.

Breaking it off with her was the only thing I could think of to try and sever the hold we had on each other.

I would wither up inside, but I could go back to keeping her safe. Not once in the eight years I watched her did anything bad happen to her.

After I forced myself into her life, she was attacked in the hallway of a bar, kidnapped by a psycho, shot, rushed into surgery and spent eight goddamn days in the hospital.

I only had a few days left before I said goodbye to the only woman I'd ever loved.

~18~

Sara

Five hours.

Five hours to go until I demanded some answers from Alek. He'd arrived back in town a day early but went straight into the office. He messaged me telling me he would be tied up all day in meetings.

More avoidance.

I couldn't go on the way I had been. It was too much. The constant worrying where our relationship stood, if he still loved me, if he still wanted to be with me. His behavior as of late was odd. It was indicative of someone who wanted out.

For the life of me, I couldn't understand why.

~~~~

"No, I haven't. Because I don't want to have the conversation with him over the phone, Alexa. I need to see his face," I whispered, doing my best to not let anyone else overhear. I would have gone into the back, but I was needed in front to man the shop until Megan was done with her current arrangement. The order was already running behind, and I didn't want to delay it any more than necessary.

As I turned to face the door, a woman walked in. Normally, I wouldn't have paid her much attention, but there was something about her which instantly set me on alert. She made eye contact with me and even scowled. Maybe she was a dissatisfied customer. Thankfully, I'd never dealt with one before, but there was a first time for everything.

"Lex, I gotta go. Talk later," I rushed as I hung up the phone. Taking a step around the counter, I approached the surly woman with my guard up, not quite knowing what to expect.

"Can I help you with something?" I asked, taking another step toward her.

She looked to be someone who'd come from money, or at the very least put on the allusion of having money. She was tall and thin, her clothes fitting her like a glove. Her dark blonde hair ran past her shoulder blades, a trendy cut which she worked at every angle. Minus the dour look on her face, she was rather beautiful, but something told me her personality was going to ruin all of it.

"You sure can, Sara," she hissed. The air of haughtiness in her tone was certainly off-putting and my guard was on high-alert.

Clenching my fists behind my back, I didn't want to let her see how she was affecting my mood. My face was expressionless but my body had tensed greatly. "Well, you appear to have me at a disadvantage. It seems you know who I am, but I have no idea who you are, Miss..." The more time I spent in her presence, the more I knew the turnout wasn't going to be pleasant.

"Bossett. Cora Bossett. Alek's fiancée."

Don't react. Don't give her the satisfaction.

Silence loomed between us. She'd certainly come out of nowhere, denying me the opportunity to prepare for such a statement. Had my relationship with Alek not been so rocky as of late, I would have laughed right in her face. But I didn't. I didn't react at all. Initially, at least.

She looked pleased with herself as she stood there glowering at me. Releasing a deep breath, I took two steps closer, fisting my hands at my sides. It was time to set her straight.

"Don't you mean ex-fiancée?" I returned her nasty scowl, glare for glare.

"No, sweetheart, *current* fiancée. We recently got back together, as I knew we would. So you see, honey, he no longer has any need for you."

I *so* wanted to punch her in the face. How dare she walk into my shop and spew such word vomit at my feet. She had some real nerve.

While anger flushed my face, my heart was breaking, a little bit for each second I stood in her presence. Before Alek started acting funny, I would have said she was crazy. There was no way in hell he'd ever take her back. He hated even talking about her. But my head was telling me to be careful. There was something amiss, and I needed to find out exactly what it was.

Don't show all your cards. Don't let your guard down.

"I don't believe you. He would never take you back, especially not after what you did to him," I spat, backing up. If I didn't put some distance between us, I was going to be hit with assault charges.

A quick look of shock crossed her face but was quickly replaced by disgust, as if I was nothing, and even having to explain anything to me at all was beneath her.

Completely ignoring my statement, she glanced around my shop in boredom. Finally, she turned her stare back in my direction.

"Woman to woman, I'm giving you the courtesy up-front to let you know Alek is done with you because he's come to his senses. Finally. He's done slumming," she declared haughtily.

It took all of my reserve not to jump on her and tackle her to the ground. I envisioned snatching her by the hair and punching her in the face, maybe even breaking her perfect little nose. My thoughts ran rampant inside my head, helping to contain some of my anger. I couldn't be arrested for merely thinking it.

"Are you done?" I was able to pull off a calm tone, even though inside I was a mess. As she flicked her hand in my direction, I caught sight of the huge rock on her ring finger. She noticed, the smirk on her face proving so.

She rotated her hand back and forth, allowing the ring to catch the light and practically blind me. "He gave this back to me last night. He said he carried it with him at all times, hoping I would come back to him someday."

When she saw my face fall, she grinned. She was done. She had accomplished what she set out to do, which was to hurt me.

"You need to leave now. Don't ever step foot in my shop again."

"Fine by me, as long as you stay away from my fiancé."

"Get out!" I shouted. She laughed as she sauntered out the front door.

As soon as she was gone, Megan walked into the front of the shop, no doubt having heard some sort of commotion. "Are you okay, Sara?"

"I will be, Megan. I will be," I repeated, not entirely believing my own words. Grabbing my purse and keys from the back room, I rushed to leave. "Megan, can you ask Matt to close up for me when he comes back? Please. Tell him I'll talk to him later."

"Sure thing," she answered as the door closed behind me.

Rushing to my car, I immediately dialed Alek's number. It went straight to voicemail. When I tried his office, his secretary told me he was in a meeting and wasn't to be disturbed for any reason.

I raced home in hopes Alexa was there so I could tell her everything.

I needed someone to talk to and since I couldn't reach the one person I needed most, my best friend was the next best choice.

~19~

Alek

Buzz. Buzz. Buzz.

What the hell is that sound? Still groggy from passing out drunk, I couldn't wrap my head around where the irritating noise was coming from. I closed my eyes again in hopes it would stop.

Buzzzzzzzzzzzz.

My lids parted again, trying to figure out where I was before I even attempted to get up. Taking a few deep breaths, the room spinning around me, I made to stand up but instead fell on my ass.

Goddamn it! That hurt.

Buzzzzz. I glanced over at my phone, but it wasn't making any noise. The only other thing it could be was the front gate.

Buzz. Buzz.

Scrambling off the floor took every ounce of energy I had left in me. Whoever was out there was going to surely get an earful from me. Unless it was Sara.

Shit! I wasn't ready to deal with our relationship yet.

I shook my head as I reached for the intercom. "Hello," I mumbled.

There was a crackling sound before I heard a woman's voice. "Hi, sweetheart. Can you let me in, please?" I couldn't place who it was, not at first, but knowing it wasn't Sara gave me a fleeting feeling of relief.

"Who is this?"

"It's me, silly. Cora. Can you please open the gate so I can come up?"

What the hell is going on? Was I still dreaming? Cora? No, it couldn't be. Why would she come back here after all this time? And why the hell was she calling me 'sweetheart' and acting as if we were still on good terms? I made it clear the last time we saw each other I wouldn't be held responsible for my actions if she ever came near me again.

Even though more than a year had passed since I laid my eyes on the despicable woman, my hatred for her was still as intense as the day I found out she aborted my child.

"Go away, Cora. I'm not letting you in." I walked away from the intercom but she was relentless.

Buzz. Buzz. Buzz. Buzz.

"If you don't let me in, Alek, I'll stay out here and lay on the horn, disturbing whatever neighbors you have."

"What do you want? Why are you here?" I mumbled.

"Let me in so we can talk, then I'll go if you still want me to. Please, sweetheart."

"Don't fucking call me that," I barked. I reached up and grabbed my neck, pulling down to assuage the tension which was quickly building. If I didn't let her in, she would definitely cause a scene, which would only make things worse. It was already almost midnight and I was fucking cranky and tired, never mind a pulsating headache was already starting to rattle my brain.

Deciding to find out what she wanted, I pushed the button to open the gate. The quicker I let her in, the quicker I could kick her out.

My doorbell rang thirty seconds later and I was instantly enraged, mainly because she was forcing me to deal with my past. Seeing her again was going to put me in a dark mood for a while to come, and I had enough on my goddamn plate.

Looking back on my time with Cora, I realized I never truly loved her, not like I loved Sara. There was simply no comparison. Which was why when she cheated on me, I was able to cut ties without a second thought. But when I found out she killed my child on purpose because I wouldn't take her back, that was the clincher which pushed me from not loving her to full-on hating her.

Ready to engage the crazy bitch, I flung open the front door. I knew I looked like I was hit by a train, but I didn't care. I was far from trying to impress her. Hell, she was lucky I didn't reach out and throttle her right where she stood.

Our eyes connected but neither one of us spoke. I was instantly hit with all of the bad memories of the last conversation we had. After a minute of simply standing there and staring at each other, she decided my rudeness was no longer tolerable. She smiled and pushed past my foreboding body, entering my personal space.

I think I was still drifting between reality and drunken stupor, the alcohol wearing off a little the more I was forced to be in Cora's presence.

After I shut the door, I turned around and realized I was only half-dressed. I'd quickly thrown on my jeans which had been tossed over the edge of the couch. They weren't even buttoned all the way, for God's sake.

She was busy taking in every facet of my home, her eyes widening the more she looked around. She was definitely impressed. If she'd only kept her legs closed, she could have had it all. But thankfully, she and my cousin Cameron were cut from the same cloth. Her betrayal essentially forced me to find my one true love.

Sara.

My thoughts flitted to the woman who was going to hate me soon enough.

"What do you want, Cora?" I pulled her attention to me, and it was a mistake. The way she drank me in actually gave me chills. I hated I was standing in front of her, shirtless and pants half-undone.

"I've come to win you back, sweetheart." She took a step toward me but I held up my hand. One look in my eyes and she knew she would be in for it if she came any closer.

Teeth clenched and jaw squared tight, I yelled out again. "Don't fucking call me that, Cora." My sudden rage startled her, and she took a step back. As I was about to tell her there was no way in hell I would ever take her back, my doorbell rang.

Now *who the hell is here?*

I turned back toward the door and as I tried to control my anger, I gripped the handle and swung it open. Standing there on my doorstep, at midnight, was Sara. She looked a little worse for wear but still stunningly beautiful. Her eyes were red and puffy. There was no argument she'd been crying.

"Sara, what are you doing here?" I was shocked she'd showed up so late but then again, I didn't blame her. It wouldn't have taken me long to barge in on her if the roles were reversed, and she was the one who was constantly blowing me off. I knew she wanted to give me some space, most likely believing the whole time I would work through whatever shit I was dealing with. "How did you get past the gate?"

Clearly my question was rude because the look on her face told me so. "It was open." Taking a deep breath, she continued with, "I know we haven't spoken a lot recently, but we really need to talk, Alek. Enough is enough already. I need to know what the hell is going on between us." A brief look of relief washed over her, and I was positive it was because she'd finally been able to broach the subject I'd been avoiding. I remained silent, not quite sure what to do or say.

She started to speak again but stopped abruptly.

Sara was no longer looking at me but instead at something behind me. Or should I say *someone* behind me? It was then I realized Cora was the someone she was staring at.

Sara's body instantly tensed, her breathing becoming shallow and rushed. Her hands clenched at her sides as she tried to control the wave of emotions rushing over her. She glanced back and forth between Cora and me, stopping to take in my half-naked, disheveled body. When her eyes finally rested on my face, she silently pleaded for an explanation. However, I couldn't give her one. I had no idea what Cora was doing there, but it didn't really matter. Knowing what was obviously running through Sara's mind was enough to put a shadow of doubt on our relationship. And in that moment, I did something I would soon regret.

I let her assume the worst.

It was a coward's way out, I knew. But I thought if she hated me, it would make it easier on her in the long run. Anger was always better than a broken heart. While fury would fuel her to push forward, a broken heart would devastate her.

It didn't take long before her eyes turned cold.

Hurt and resentment danced with sadness and rage.

The woman standing before me was quickly becoming someone I didn't recognize, and I hated the fact I was the man responsible.

"Sara..." I only called out her name. Nothing more. There was so much I wanted to say to her, but I didn't.

While I knew her heart was breaking, she remained stoic, simply stepping closer. Tears had broken free and cascaded down her cheeks. Then I saw the emotion in her eyes switch to full-on anger. "I hate you!" she seethed before turning and fleeing to her car.

I knew she meant what she said. She truly hated me.

Join the club. I hate myself right about now.

My soul ached. None of my actions could justify hurting her the way I had, and it wasn't only that night. I'd slowly been withdrawing from her, tearing open her heart and confusing the hell out of her. I made her second-guess our relationship. I even made her second-guess my love for her.

I flip-flopped back and forth so many times about what I should do.

Well, it seemed my decision was just made for me.

I could only hope in time she would forgive me, and although anger was the better emotion to have then, I hoped it didn't end up consuming her.

Once I closed the door, I spun around only to catch Cora leering at my naked chest. The woman was unbelievable. I was still in shock she showed up at my house.

Without giving me the time to mourn the loss of my relationship, Cora started in with her shit.

"You should know Sara and I had a little chat today." She smirked.

No. She didn't say what I think she did. The alcohol is messing with me.

The sneer on her face challenged me.

"What the fuck did you say?"

Noticing the look of pure rage on my face caused her to retreat. She stuttered over her next words. "I went...t...to see her today at her little s...shop." She was pissed I'd made her stumble over her words, so she squared her shoulders before continuing with the rest of her story. "I told her we were back together, so she should leave you alone."

She knew her mistake as soon as the last syllable left her lying lips.

My movements were too quick for her to react. Snatching her up, I crushed her bony body to mine. We were practically nose to nose. Gripping her arms tight, I yelled in her face. "You...bitch! Don't you EVER step foot near her again. Do you understand me? EVER!" I'd never raised a hand to a woman in my life, but I was finding it difficult to control myself. All I wanted to do was squeeze the life from her. After everything she'd done to me, she added hurting Sara to her list. Although, I could add myself into that category, as well.

"Alek, you're hurting me." She tried to struggle in my grasp, but it was useless. I made sure to hold on to her longer so she knew how serious I was.

As soon as I released her, she stumbled backward. "Alek, baby. I think we owe it to ourselves to give our relationship another try and work this out. We were so good together. And I'm sorry...about everything. Please."

This bitch is crazy.

I shook my head in amazement. I actually felt sorry for the pathetic woman standing in front of me. Not only was she delusional, but she was insane if she thought I would ever take her back.

The longer she stood in front of me, the more I suspected something else was up. There was no way she truly thought she could win me over. So, what else could it be?

I was lost until something occurred to me. I saw the way her eyes lit up when she walked into my house. She came from money, so she shouldn't have been so impressed.

Then a light bulb went off.

"You need money, don't you, Cora?" My words made her turn away for a split-second. *Bingo.* She was here for a handout. But something else didn't add up, either. No way would Cora show up at my house, unannounced in the middle of the night, confess she told Sara what she did and still expect me to give her what she wanted.

No. Someone put her up to it. Someone had convinced her that her crazy plan would work. Someone who knew how desperate she was.

And I had an idea exactly who it was. Only one other person I knew had the balls to back such a foolish plan: the guy who was still trying to mess with me. Well, I'd had enough. I was going to take care of him once and for all.

"Cameron put you up to this, didn't he?" She looked stunned I'd actually figured it out. "Didn't he?" I roared.

I didn't give her a chance to deny it before I seized her wrist and dragged her toward the front door. As soon as I opened it, I shoved her outside. She didn't fall, but she did stumble. "Go fucking ask *him* for a handout because you won't get one from me. And Cora? If you *ever* come near me or Sara again, you'll regret it. Trust me."

As the door latched shut on my past, I couldn't help but wonder what my future would bring.

~~~~

For two months I'd been drowning in grief, and I couldn't take it any longer. Sara missing from my life was like my heart being torn from my chest. I knew I was the one who sliced it out, but at the time I thought it was for the best. For her. I wasn't so sure anymore.

I'd witnessed her version of living over the past eight weeks. I didn't even know if she was aware I was watching, but I was. Of course I was; I had to make sure she was all right. Well, physically, at least. It was the whole reason I'd basically broken it off with her.

A reason I'd instantly regretted.

She was sullen and removed, never venturing out except to her shop then back home again. I didn't even think she went to the grocery store, most likely relying on Alexa to take care of all the mundane daily tasks.

Physically, although still the most beautiful woman I'd ever laid eyes on, she lost weight. Her face was forever saddened and most times, her eyes were reddened and swollen. I hated I was the person solely responsible for turning her into a shell of her former self.

Amongst her sadness, however, was deep-seated anger. I had no doubt in my heart she hated me. She told me so. And even if she hadn't meant it that night, enough time had gone by for those feelings to have been cemented deep inside of her. I would rather her hate me than be torn apart by what I did to her. Yes, anger was a much better emotion to wrangle with. It provided a blanket of comfort, something to ward off the knives trying to weave themselves into one's very soul.

I knew of such things because anger sheathed me every day. I hated myself and tried to find comfort in the bottom of a bottle. Each night, I'd drown my sorrows with the burning liquid. It lasted for only a short while, then I was back to harboring regret and anger in the morning. I was slowly killing myself; every day I didn't redeem myself was another proverbial nail in the coffin.

One day, I'd finally woken up with hope in my heart. I was going to attempt to see Sara. I needed to try and explain why I'd done what I did. Knowing her, she definitely wouldn't make it easy for me and I wouldn't want her to. Hell, I didn't know if she would even talk to me again. Ever. But I had to try.

The tracking device on her phone was still active. I didn't know if she forgot about it or if she secretly hoped I'd use it someday. I was hoping for the latter. I wouldn't show up at Full Bloom or her apartment. I didn't want to disturb any kind of solace she'd been able to find at either place. I was admittedly an asshole, but I wasn't cruel. *Although some might beg to differ.*

The next time she ventured anywhere else, though, I was going to *accidentally* run into her. I was hoping she still had love in her heart for me, even if she hated me. The connection we shared was too powerful for her feelings to disappear altogether.

It was what I would keep repeating to myself until the day I'd finally be able to see her again.

~20~

Sara

Three months had passed since I'd seen or heard from Alek. It was a struggle each single day to try and function like a normal human being. With every ounce of strength I possessed, I'd drag my sorry ass out of bed in the morning. No more than four hours of sleep rescued me from my reality, so not only was I an emotional wreck, but my physical self had taken a beating, as well. I'd lost weight, my hair wasn't as vibrant and there were dark circles under my eyes. *Thank God for concealer.* But I didn't care. I was simply living to exist.

There were many times I'd chastised myself for ever becoming involved with Alek. Going in, I knew it was too good to be true. I feared he'd break my heart...and he did. He was good, though. Telling me he loved me, acting as if my safety was his number one concern...I felt like a fool.

The last time I'd seen him played over and over in my head. That awful woman standing in his house, him practically naked. What were they doing before I rang his doorbell? The mere thought was torture, so I tried not to think about it but sometimes, when I was feeling really low, I took it there.

Seeing the anger laced in his eyes had confused me, though. I wasn't sure if he was upset before he opened the door or once he'd realized it was me on the other side. There were too many what-ifs. I would never truly know the full story, and I had to chalk it up to nothing more than an extremely heartbreaking life lesson.

Don't fall for hot, rich men. And surely don't give that same man a second chance after he reveals he'd been watching you for eight years.

But even that, I came to understand. After he'd explained everything, mentioning his promise to my grandmother, a woman who I loved more than anything, I saw the situation for what it was. A young man trying to help ease an elderly woman's heart, but also trying to make up for not being able to save his own sister.

Confusion had become my go-to emotion as of late. It was better to hide behind than devastation and raging anger.

Alexa was the only one I'd truly confided in. Matt wouldn't understand. All he would want to do was hunt down Alek and try to teach him a lesson, and I didn't want to put him in any kind of situation where he could possibly be harmed. Alek had grown used to Matt's place in my life. Dare I say he even began to like him? I wasn't sure how he would react if Matt came at him, though, and it was a risk I wasn't willing to take.

The more days that crept by, the more numb I became. I didn't know if it was my survival instincts kicking in, but I feared if something didn't change soon, I would simply die inside and never feel anything ever again.

No happiness.

No anger.

No sadness.

Nothing.

I smiled politely to those around me and uttered "Fine" when they asked how I was doing. But I never told the truth. I always lied.

~ ~ ~ ~

"Are we still going out tonight, Sara? Please, tell me you're not going to back out again. You haven't been out of this house, besides to work, in way too long." Alexa stood by the couch with her hands on her hips, glaring down at me. I knew she was upset with me, but I couldn't find it inside me to care much.

She was doing her absolute best to help pull me from my dark depression. Because I was so thankful to have such a wonderful friend in my life, I decided to stick to our plans for once. I couldn't imagine having any fun, but I would fake it like I had been for the past few months.

"Sara? Did you hear me? Are you going to cancel on me again?" My dear friend was frustrated, and I didn't blame her.

I tore my eyes away from the mindless TV show and looked up at her. A small, forced smile tipped my lips. "Yes, I'm still going." She acted as if I'd told her I cured cancer. Her smile was huge, but she quickly regained her composure.

Sitting down next to me, she placed her hand on my arm. "Don't be mad, but you need to eat. You're losing too much weight, and it isn't healthy."

Gingerly glancing down at my thinner frame, I half-smiled. I had lost at least twenty pounds because I didn't bother to nourish myself. There were days when I hardly ate anything at all, waiting until dinnertime to have something simple, like a piece of fruit. Both Matt and Alexa took turns trying to force-feed me, but their efforts were wasted.

"I know, Lex. I promise I'll eat something before we go."

"Not a piece of fruit, Sara. I want you to eat something real, something nutritious. You have to stop abusing your body like this or you'll end up really sick."

She was a thousand percent right and I knew it. I had no energy as it was. My hair and skin looked dull, and there was a constant beat-down look in my eyes.

"I'll eat a good meal, I promise."

She looked skeptical at first, and then a smile encroached on her beautiful face as she sat there grinning at me.

"I know you will. Because I'm going to make us both something to eat. Plus, if our stomachs are full, we can drink more." She laughed as she made her way to the kitchen and started pulling ingredients from the refrigerator.

She ended up making us chicken francese, veggies and a side salad with all of the fixings. I tried to muster enough of an appetite to eat all of it, but my stomach had shrunk drastically and I could only manage half.

I sat back after eating and had to admit I felt a little better already. A small surge of energy pumped through me because of the meal she'd forced me to eat.

"Thanks for dinner. I'm going to take a shower now and start getting ready. You don't plan on staying out too late, do you?"

"Sara..." she warned. "Don't worry about how late we're going to be. The only thing I want you to focus on is enjoying yourself. For once."

"Okay, okay. I promise I'll try and enjoy myself. 'Fake it till you make it', right? Isn't that the saying?"

"Yes, it is," she replied, giving me a hug before she turned around to clean up from dinner.

~21~

Sara

We ended up at a smaller, local bar. I told Alexa I wasn't ready to be around a large group of people. She understood and was grateful I'd ventured outside our apartment at all.

An hour in and I'd already consumed a couple of drinks. I wasn't drunk by any means, but the familiar twinge of lightheartedness was upon me and I welcomed it with open arms.

Alexa and I were in mid-conversation when Braden came walking through the front door. Since there weren't too many patrons, he'd been able to locate us rather quickly.

"Hi, Sara. How are you?" he greeted. An undercurrent of sympathy swirled around his words as he addressed me.

"Fine, Braden. How are you?" Simple pleasantries passed between us as usual. I liked him. Besides being a nice guy, he was head-over-heels for my best friend. He was intense, but his love for her was undeniable.

I had that once. Or so I thought.

"Good, good." He locked eyes with his woman and I knew something wasn't right. Palpable tension enveloped them, but neither one gave way to what was wrong. After more uncomfortable silence, she was the first to speak.

"I thought you said you were working late tonight," she said with an air of aloofness.

"Yeah, well, I figured you were more important than the papers I was going over with my assistant." He tried to smile but faltered.

"I'm surprised you were able to tear yourself away from *her*."

Oh, no.

Braden's hand rested on her elbow. Leaning in, he softly spoke. "Can we not do this here? In public? If you still have an issue, I would be more than happy to go somewhere more private so we can discuss it like adults. Instead of throwing out insinuations." Her breath paused as she quickly made eye contact with me.

Apparently, there was some sort of issue going on between them, and I was guessing it had everything to do with his assistant.

"I'm not going anywhere with you. Sara and I were having a great time until you showed up to dampen the mood."

He turned toward me and tried to force yet another smile before he focused all of his attention on Alexa. He leaned in close and whispered something in her ear. She had no reaction until suddenly a blush crept up her neck and broke out across her cheeks. He leaned back and cocked his brow, waiting for her to make a move. Within seconds, she hopped off her seat. He reached for her hand and she swatted him away but continued to allow him to usher her into a private hallway.

I remembered being in similar situations with Alek. *Damn it.* Why did thoughts of him have to infiltrate my brain? I'd been doing well so far, only thinking about him twice before Alexa was able to successfully distract me. But she left me alone to dwell on the one man who had consumed me for months.

Glancing toward the hallway where they had disappeared, I prayed they would settle their issue and come back out to join me. A couple of minutes passed and still nothing. Running my fingers over the coolness of my glass, I picked it up and took a sip. The drink soothed my worries, allowing me some time to swallow its tantalizing numbness.

Deciding to take in my surroundings, my eyes roamed all over the small space. There weren't many people there, but that was fine with me. Two guys were playing pool in the far corner. Four women were sitting in a booth, laughing as if they didn't have a care in the world. One guy was trying to score for the evening, running his finger up and down a woman's arm. She looked interested.

Lucky bastards. I miss him. I miss being wrapped in his arms. I miss the way his lips taste.

Deciding more liquor would squelch those insane feelings, I gulped down the rest of my drink. As I placed the glass back on the bar, I caught movement to my right, near the front door.

My eyes grazed over the man leaning against the wall. Even though I'd only looked at him for a split-second, I knew who it was immediately.

I blinked repeatedly, praying the alcohol was causing me to hallucinate.

But he was real.

Just when I'd started to feel a bit of humanity pulse through my veins, it was destroyed by the mere sight of him.

He didn't see me at first because he was busy checking out the other patrons. . Was it a mere coincidence he was there? Was he waiting for someone else? Another woman? Was he meeting Cora? The thought alone broke my heart all over again.

A crazy thought entered my mind, but I quickly shoved it aside. I'd totally forgotten about the tracker he installed on my cell phone after the kidnapping. There was no way he still kept tabs on me. *Are you kidding? Look who you're talking about.* The thought he was there for me was ludicrous. *But why, then? After months of silence, why now?*

Then a thought barreled forth, almost knocking me off my stool. That night was the first time I'd gone out since our relationship ended—other than work, of course.

Hope filled me but quickly dispelled any such feeling. I wasn't going to allow him to play with my emotions any longer.

"Sara? Are you ready to go home now?" Alexa asked, barreling out from the back of the hallway. She was still upset. It was obvious the issue between her and her man hadn't been resolved. If anything, it had only intensified. Braden was but a few paces behind her, looking none too pleased.

Swinging my head around, I locked eyes with Alek. He'd heard Lex call my name and honed right in on me.

I was way too fragile to have any kind of communication with him, verbal or otherwise. I broke eye contact, seized Alexa by her wrist and leaned into her ear, shaking the whole time.

"Help me," were the only words I spoke.

She turned her head so she could look at me. "What's the matter, Sara? Why are you shaking? Did someone say something to you?" Forgetting her argument with Braden, she summoned him closer to us.

"What's the matter? Is there anything I can do?" he asked pensively. Reaching out, he touched my shoulder, trying his best to comfort me.

I must've looked like a fool, shaking for what appeared to be no reason at all. But there *was* a reason, and he was standing across the bar staring at me. He was also looking at Braden, boring holes right through him. Clearly he wasn't sure if Braden was with me or Alexa. Although Alek knew of Alexa's boyfriend, he'd never met him before.

Every fiber of my being wished Alek was being bombarded with thoughts of me having sex with the man touching me. *Sorry, Lex.* I would love nothing more than for him to be racked with images of us writhing around together. I hoped he envisioned me screaming out in ecstasy as Braden made me come.

A small smile crooked the corners of my mouth. I must have looked like a crazy person, but I didn't care. I would grab on to anything if it meant saving me from completely shutting down.

"Sara? Can you hear me?" Lex shouted.

Coming back into my tortured reality, I answered her. "Yeah, sorry. I want to leave. Now!"

I glanced back toward Alek and my best friend followed to see who I was looking at. She gasped as she leaned in closer, throwing her arm around my shoulder.

Taking a deep breath, I straightened my spine and prepared for a confrontation. There was something about the way he was staring at me which told me there was no way I was going to walk by him without him saying something. Why did he have to be near the front door, of all places?

"I wonder if there's a back way out of this place," Alexa muttered. She knew exactly why I was acting weird. She wanted to save me from having to walk past him, as well.

"No, that's okay. I have to face him sooner or later, I suppose." My words sounded strong, but I was anything but. I was quaking inside, fearful I would break down in front of him and scream for him to give me an explanation.

Braden continued to stand next to me, but he looked confused. I saw Lex mouth *ex-boyfriend* as we advanced toward the door.

Alek shifted from one foot to the other the closer we got. His eyes switched from looking at me to the ground, then to the other patrons before landing back on my face. *He's nervous.* The simple fact he didn't know how to act around me either gave me some comfort.

As I approached him, my heart hammered away inside my chest. Beads of sweat broke out along my forehead and my hands were suddenly clammy. I found it difficult to breathe, and I was praying I didn't experience a panic attack right in front of him.

Suddenly, I found myself standing inches away from him. Part of his body was blocking the exit and while he continued to shift from side to side, he never moved enough for me to walk out the door.

Then he spoke.

"Sara. How are you?" The deep timber of his voice cut straight through me. *Damn him.*

I honestly didn't know what to say to him, so I remained silent. It was safer that way.

He didn't utter another word, but he didn't move, either. A look of pain cascaded over his gorgeous face. His eyes slowly roamed my body, but not so slow as to be disrespectful. No doubt he'd taken notice of my weight loss.

Blowing out a breath of frustration, I sternly commanded, "Move." I couldn't even say his name aloud.

"Sara, please, can I talk to you?" He reached out to touch me, but I moved back. His bottom lip disappeared between his teeth, a nervous habit he'd picked up toward the end of our relationship.

"Move!" I shouted that time, hoping he would have the decency to let me pass. But still, he did nothing. Until Braden interfered.

"You heard her. Get the fuck out of her way."

Glancing to the side, I witnessed the tick of Braden's jaw as he fought the urge to tackle Alek. He loved Alexa, and since I was her best friend, he believed he had a duty to protect me, as well.

"This doesn't have anything to do with you, so back off!" Alek shouted, the look on his face suddenly changing. He was gearing up for battle, sizing up who he probably thought was his competition. The fact Braden wrapped his arm around my waist and pulled me into him certainly sealed any ideas Alek had about the man.

Alek didn't miss a thing, recognizing the sign of possession right away. He knew it all too well.

I'd have to thank them both later on for letting the charade continue, although I was sure Braden thought he was doing nothing more than protecting his girlfriend's best friend.

"If you don't move out of her way right now, you and I are going to have a real big problem." Braden straightened himself to his full six-foot-three frame. He was pretty much head to head with Alek, in height, weight and presence.

I had to dispel the situation before anything escalated.

"It's okay," I assured them both, all the while continuing to look directly at Alek. "He'll move because he doesn't want to cause a scene and upset me. Right, Alek?" His name sounded foreign on my tongue.

"Yeah, sure," he asserted. A few seconds later, he moved over and allowed all of us to pass by. Braden knocked into Alek's shoulder, sneering at him the entire time.

Note to self: don't get on Braden's bad side.

Once outside, Braden informed us he was going to bring his car around. Thank goodness we didn't have to wait for a cab. The faster I got out of there, the better.

We weren't outside for twenty seconds before Alek came sauntering out of the bar, walking toward me with an intent look on his face.

Oh, God. I can't do this. I can't do this.

Reaching for Alexa to help steady me, she looked confused until she saw what was happening. She was on him faster than I could even say anything.

"Alek, don't you dare," she warned. "Don't you think you've done enough damage? Do you get your kicks out of hurting my friend?" She took a step closer, the look on her face set to kill. "I suggest you leave before Braden gets back."

Thank the heavens above Alexa didn't reference him as her boyfriend. She let it hang out there as if he might've been with me.

"I need a minute to speak to you, Sara." He didn't even bother responding to Alexa. He was solely focused on me, and nothing else.

I knew it was only a matter of minutes before we took off for home, so I cut Alexa off before she started in on him again.

"It's okay, Lex. We're leaving soon anyway, so I'll be okay."

"You sure?"

"Yeah, I'm sure. Thanks." I gave her a faint smile, but the look in my eyes told her I needed to talk to him.

"Okay. I'm right over here if you need me." She squeezed my shoulder before turning her gaze back on the man in front of me. "I got my eye on you, Devera, so don't try anything funny." She stepped back to give us some privacy.

Standing up straight, I inhaled a big breath of air, hoping it would give me the strength I needed right then. It was hard to look directly at him, but I mustered the courage in order to have my say and be done with it. "What could you possibly have to say to me?"

He dove right in, realizing he didn't have much time at all. "Sara, first I want to tell you how sorry I am for hurting you. I hope you believe it was never my intention. I swear. Hurting you was the last thing I wanted to do." When I opened my mouth to interject, he cut me off. "I know it's so cliché, but it's true. But I promise you there *is* a good reason for it."

"Yeah, what might that be? What possible reason could you have had to cut my heart out and stomp all over it?" Anger gripped my insides, threatening to explode all over him if he didn't end our little conversation soon.

Having the decency to know I was ready to erupt, he looked away quickly before catching my eye again. "Do you think we can go somewhere and talk? If you give me a chance, I can explain everything." When he saw the blank look on my face, he faltered. But it didn't last long before he was back at it. "I'm so sorry," he said, reaching out to touch my hand. "If you just give me the chance to explain, I can make it all right."

Instant flashbacks bombarded me. I was in the same exact predicament with him before when he was begging for a chance to explain why I'd found a file full of pictures of me in his possession. "Boy, isn't this déjà vu?" I chided, a disgusted look contorting my face.

He at least had the decency to look embarrassed, knowing full well he was always asking a lot from me, putting me through the emotional wringer.

"I know...I know. But please, I need you to trust me."

I'd had enough, and if I didn't tell him exactly what I thought of him, I was going to end up taking out my anger on everyone else besides the person who deserved it.

"Trust you?" I bellowed. "Why the *fuck* would I ever trust you again? You can rot in Hell for all I care. The hate I have for you helps me sleep at night." Somewhere along the way, my hands had clenched into tight balls, my fingernails digging into the flesh of my palms in order to keep from ripping his face off. "How about you, Alek? How do you sleep at night knowing you messed up the best thing to ever happen to you?"

I was lying. I didn't hate him. I loved him, but I would never utter the words. I would not play the victim and let him see how much he hurt me. No, I wouldn't give him the satisfaction. I cried in front of him once when he broke my heart, on the steps of his home three months back. I wouldn't do it again. Anger was my new best friend, and I was going to lean on it to help me through my encounter with him.

Not knowing what else to do, he crushed the distance between us, all the while whispering, "I'm so sorry, baby." I knew if I ever allowed him to touch me, I would be in big trouble. I talked a good game, but I was a mess on the inside. And like a predator, he knew it. For every step he took toward me, I took one back, until eventually my body was pressed against a car parked on the sidewalk.

Great! I'm trapped.

He placed an arm on either side of me, resting his hands on the hood of the vehicle, effectively caging me in. He was so close to me, his warm breath fanned across my heated face. I'd cried too many tears over Alek only to be undone with one of his soul-searching stares.

"Baby," he pleaded, his eyes offering up his sincerest apologies.

Don't look at him. Averting my eyes, I glanced everywhere but at the man in front of me. But there came a point when I could no longer ignore him. When my eyes locked back on his, something happened. Something I was trying to avoid but was powerless to stop. The way he looked at me washed away the past months without him. My entire world ceased to exist, ultimately leaving me defenseless against him. He was my drug, and I hadn't realized how much I was itching for a fix until he was so daringly close to me.

Without warning, he leaned in as if he was going to kiss me. My body was rigid, my mind warring between allowing him to consume me and slapping him across the face. Thankfully, neither of those scenarios happened. As he was effectively pinning me against the car, a thought raced through my head. Yes, I still loved him, but did I believe he still loved me? How could someone dismiss another from their life so easily if they were, in fact, in love? *It's not possible.* No, he still *desired* me; that much was true. But *love?* He didn't love me. And once the acknowledgment sank in, I found the strength I needed to push him away from me.

Once my hands found their way to his chest, he looked like he'd been shocked. A shudder vibrated through his body as his breath caught in his throat. I found my opportunity, pushed him back a step and escaped his emotionally torturous imprisonment. "I won't do this to myself again, Alek," I yelled over my shoulder as I rushed toward Alexa.

"Sara, please. I promise I'll make it up to you. I'm sorry!" he shouted as the distance separated us from each other.

I made sure not to make eye contact with him as we passed in the car. He was still standing on the sidewalk, but I wouldn't allow any more vulnerability to corrupt me.

My body ached for his touch.

But my brain told me I did the right thing. Breaking away from him was the only way the rest of my fragile heart could heal.

Finally.

~22~

Sara

"I don't want to talk about it, Lex. Please...let it go. I know you're worried about me, but it's better if I work on forgetting." I was trying to busy myself with folding my laundry, but she was making it near impossible, standing in my bedroom in full-on interrogation mode.

"Sara, it's been a week since you saw him and you haven't said a single thing about it. I'm thankful you're not sitting here crying over him, but it's kind of freaking me out you don't want to say anything at all about what happened. Don't you need some kind of closure or something?"

"That *was* my closure. It was my final goodbye to the man who both saved and destroyed me. He made me feel again after so long, but he also tore my heart out after he had his fill, tossing me aside once he had no more use for me." My mind instantly reverted back to the night I showed up at his house and caught him with *her*.

"Well, I'm here if you need me," she offered, picking up one of my shirts, making a face and tossing it back on my bed. Good ol' Lex. She made me laugh right then, and it was something I definitely needed.

I walked toward my dresser to put some of my clothes away. Reaching for her hand, I drew her close to me and gave her a big hug. "Thanks for worrying about me. Love you."

"Love you, too, girl." She walked across the room and was awkwardly quiet. At first, I wasn't paying much attention to her but when she simply stood there staring at me, it became a little weird.

"Are you okay? Did you want to talk about something else?" I prodded before heading into my closet to hang some of my shirts.

"Remember you love me," she teased.

Oh, Lord.

"What did you do?" Before I let her answer, I spouted, "You better not have been in contact with him, or so help me, God, Alexa Bearnheart."

"Who are you talking about?"

"Alek," I gritted through clenched teeth.

There was no hesitation on her part. "Fuck no. I learned my lesson the last time. I told you I would always take your side, no matter what. Fool me once..." she chanted.

"Then what is it you have to tell me?"

"Um...nothing big. Just...uh..." She stumbled over her words, which was so unlike her.

"Spit it out, Lex."

And spit it out she did, all in one quick breath. "Braden is bringing a colleague of his to the restaurant opening on Saturday night."

"What?" It took me a minute to try and figure out why she would be so nervous, and then it dawned on me. "I hope you guys are not setting me up on a blind date." When she averted her eyes, looking anywhere and everywhere but at my stunned face, I knew it was true. Sure, I admitted closing the *Alek* chapter of my life, but I was in no way ready to date anyone else. Not for a very long time to come.

When she still didn't speak, I made sure to crowd her personal space, forcing her to give me an answer. "Is it a blind date, Alexa?"

"Yes." One simple word, but one I didn't want to hear.

"Does this guy know it's a blind date?"

"Well...sort of. Hell, I don't know. I don't know what Braden told him exactly. But I'm sure he hinted at it, Sara."

"Well, I'm not going now, so you can forget about it." I stalked away from her and into the bathroom. It was late and I needed to take a shower before bed.

"You *are* going because I'm not allowing you to chicken out." When she sensed her words were falling on deaf ears, she followed me into the bathroom and was the one crowding my personal space in return.

"You listen here. I love you as if you were my own sister, but I've listened to you cry for three months over that asshole. I've been your shoulder to lean on, talked you down from your bouts of hysteria, and have been there for you in every other way possible. Even force-feeding you so you didn't starve to death. I was happy to do it. All of it. But right now, you have an opportunity to start living again and meet some new people, and damn it, you're going to do it. You don't have to marry the guy, you don't even have to sleep with him, but you *will* put on your big-girl panties and enjoy one night out with friends. See where the night takes you." She stunned me speechless. "Do you understand me?" she demanded.

How could I argue with anything she'd said? I couldn't, so I gave in. "Fine."

"Good. Now, is there anything else you want to talk about?" She laughed, knowing she'd essentially trapped me into a night of forced fun.

"Nope, I think you about covered it." I quickly learned it was best not to fight her. She'd made some really good points, and because she was such a great friend, I decided to go along with her plans. Humor her. *Who knows? Maybe I'll actually end up having a good time for once.*

~23~

Alek

Drunk.

I was drunk yet again.

It seemed the only thing I was good at following through with recently was downing large amounts of alcohol. As I lay on the couch, I couldn't help but think back to the previous week. Apparently, I loved to torture myself.

It'd been seven long days since my planned encounter with Sara. She looked beautiful, of course, but her distress enveloped her, making her look tired. Weight loss was the first thing I noticed. She was too thin, obviously the result of her not eating. When I was close enough, I saw the dark circles hovering under her eyes. She did her best to cover them up, but it didn't really work.

My heart leapt when she finally made eye contact with me. I lost my breath for a few seconds. No matter how much time went by, it would do nothing to squelch the sizzling desire which passed between us whenever we were close. I knew my presence was going to affect her. Hell, it affected me more than I ever wanted to admit. But I had to see her. I was going out of my mind not being able to talk to her. I wanted to beg for forgiveness so many times but never found my opportunity until that night.

I knew I was a dick for trapping her the way I did, but she wouldn't listen to me otherwise. Seeing the anger in her eyes was a good thing; it meant she still had some sort of feeling toward me. When I leaned into her, I thought I caught a glimpse of desire there as well, but I didn't have enough time to find out before she started yelling at me. I wouldn't lie and say her words didn't hurt me, but I deserved all she had to give and then some. Wanting nothing more than to tame her rage with a kiss, I knew better than to push her too far.

Winning her back again was going to be my biggest feat. I wasn't sure if she would even give me a third chance, because that was exactly what it was.

My *third* chance.

I tried my hardest not to think about it, but I couldn't forget the way that asshole claimed Sara...right in front of me. Who the hell did he think he was, touching her so intimately, clearly showing his sign of possession? I knew what he was doing because I'd exhibited the same behavior when she was mine. I knew it was Neanderthal-like but I was letting every other man in the room know she was taken.

She was mine.

Except she wasn't mine anymore.

I was forced from my thoughts when the sound of my phone cut through the air. My hand dangled over the couch, desperately trying to search for the damn thing. Once I'd found it, I did my best to see who was calling, but my vision was blurry. *Fuck it! I'll answer it blind.*

"Hello," I slurred down the line.

"What the fuck, man? You missed our meeting. Again," Kael berated on the other end. I heard him huffing into the phone. What? Did he miraculously think I would get my shit together simply because he was annoyed with me? "You've haven't been yourself ever since you made that stupid, self-sacrificing choice." He remained quiet, clearly trying to give me some time to react. I chose not to respond. "I told you not to do it, Alek. I told you not to make any rash decisions, to think about it before you decided to cut her out of your life."

"I *did* think about it!" I finally yelled in response. "It's all I fucking thought about, drunk and sober, night and day. It was the best choice for her. At the time."

"Yeah. You keep telling yourself that. Keep trying to convince yourself what you did was the best thing for her." Kael was obviously pissed off at me. He knew I was hurting, trying to assuage my pain with alcohol. Which was exactly why I missed yet another one of our meetings.

"I don't want to talk about this anymore, Kael. She won't even talk to me. I've tried, but she hates me." I blew out a drunken breath of air. "She hates me, Kael. What am I going to do?"

"Wait. When did you try to talk to her?"

"Last week, but some asshole had his hands all over my woman. He didn't want her to talk to me, but I fooled him. I made him disappear so I could pin her against the car." The scene played out in my head, but the words spewing from my mouth made everything sound weird.

"Jesus Christ, Alek. Did you attack her? So help me, if you harmed her in any way, I'll kick your ass myself." He was seething, his anger palpable even through the phone.

"How could you think I would ever do that?" Even drunk, I was offended he thought so little of me. But then again, I'd been drunk for the majority of the past three months, so it seemed he had cause to worry. "I love her, Kael. I love her so much," I cried into the phone. If I knew anything about my good friend, I knew he was shaking his head at me.

"Listen. Here is what you're going to do. And so help me, if you don't, I'm coming over there and we're going to have it out."

"You can't take me," I teased, a smile on my drunken face because I knew he was being funny.

"Yes, I can, especially since you'd probably be in one of your stupors."

"Whatever. What do you want me to do?" Grasping the back of my neck, I pulled at the tight muscles, throwing my head back to try and relieve some of the pain. My little movement almost caused me to fall over.

"I need you to sober up. I had to delay the designer again and she didn't seem too pleased, muttering something about other jobs and shit. I can't move it again. If we want this place up and running by the projected date, you have to get your priorities straight and put down the damn bottle."

I pulled the phone away from my ear because all of a sudden, he was yelling. Or had he been doing that the entire time? "I know. I got it.-I heard you."

"Good. Now, what time are you swinging by my office today? We still have to go over a couple more items before we can even give her the green light to start."

"I'll be by around two." I was so done with our conversation. If I heard one more of Kael's lectures, I was going to lose it.

After hanging up the phone, I stumbled over to the desk, put the lid back on my new best friend Jack and headed upstairs to clean up.

~~~~

I arrived at Kael's office with five minutes to spare. I felt like shit and was sure I looked like it, too. If given the opportunity, I was sure my dear friend would be the first to point it out to me as well, trying to solidify his point about how out of control I'd become.

His office door swung open and I was surprised to see Adara sauntering my way, a satisfied smile spread wide across her beautiful face. When her eyes met mine, her smile faltered for a brief moment. Still walking toward me, she opened her arms without hesitation and I walked right into them. It was nice to feel a woman's touch again, although her embrace was in no way sexual, simply comforting.

"Oh, Alek, honey." She kissed my cheek and hugged me tighter. "How are you?"

"I'm fine." When my simple statement did nothing to satiate her, I tried to lie to her again. "Really."

"Uh-huh," she appeased. "You have to come over to the house. We would love to have you." We were still wrapped up in our embrace when her husband strode out from his office, stopping for a split-second when he saw us. I knew he trusted me a thousand percent, but the sight of another man touching his wife was enough for him to still become a little riled. I didn't blame him, either. I would have reacted the same exact way if he was touching Sara, even though she wasn't mine any longer.

"All right, all right. Enough groping my wife, Devera. Hands off." He smiled, but it didn't reach his eyes. He'd broken out the tough love bit with me earlier, so as payback I decided to have a little fun with him.

I grabbed Adara, pressing my hands to the small of her back, and drew her closer to me. None of our intimate areas were touching, but he got the message. "I'm only too happy to accept the kind of comforting your wife is willing to give me," I taunted. I saw the look of irritation flicker in his eyes, but I kept going. Plus, Adara was chuckling the whole time I incessantly teased her husband. "Be a friend, Kael. I'm hurting here. I need this." As I leaned closer to whisper something in her ear, our hug was ripped apart.

"Not fucking funny, man." He shot a disbelieving look at his wife, but it did nothing to squash the laughter which emanated from her lips. "Maybe if you weren't such an asshole, you would have your own woman to molest." I knew he was trying to bait me, but I was too wrapped up in the teasing moment to reflect fully on his words.

"All right already. Stop fighting over little ol' me." Adara laughed. She reached up, cupped the side of Kael's face and tenderly gazed at him. "I'll see you at home, honey." Giving him a quick kiss, she turned around to walk away but not before giving me a friendly wink over her shoulder. My friend sure was one lucky son of a bitch.

If I waited for him to stop leering after his own wife, I'd be there all day. Pushing past him, I walked into his office, grabbed a bottled water from his fridge and plopped down on the couch.

We only had a limited amount of days left to hash out all the details before our newest project was set to go. *So I'd better put my head on straight before Kael makes good on his promise and tries to kick my ass.*

~24~

Sara

The night had finally arrived. I'd reluctantly agreed to accompany Alexa and Braden to Verdana's new opening, where essentially they were setting me up on a blind date. *At least I'll eat some good food.*

I'd been taking better care of myself, eating more to help replenish the weight I'd lost. I'd even started running. Each time my foot hit the pavement, it helped to clear away the cobwebs from my head. Running had quickly become an escape for me. Plus, it was great exercise.

"Girl, are you almost ready?" Alexa yelled from the living room. "Braden's gonna be here any minute to pick us up." Hell must have frozen over for her to actually be ready before me. But then again, I was taking my sweet-ass time, as I did with most things lately.

What's the rush? What am I hurrying toward?

"I'll be right there." Semi-satisfied with the image staring back at me, I snatched my purse off the bed, flicked off my bedroom light and headed out to the front room.

We arrived at the newest grand opening right on time, bypassing the long line of patrons patiently waiting to enter. Braden was able to secure us VIP status, something I didn't even know existed for restaurants. We were led right to a private section, a waitress in tow as we ordered our drinks, and settled in for what would hopefully be a good night. Braden's friend James was going to be joining us in a little while. At least I had some time to loosen up before my nerves took hold.

"This place is amazing," I raved, my eyes roaming over the fixtures of the expansive building. We were surrounded by white and stainless steel which was quite masculine, but there were splashes of sensual colors mixed throughout. Beautiful artwork decorated the walls while exquisite candles complemented the center of each table. The flickering flames added to the ambiance of the restaurant, making it appear more cozy and intimate.

"Yeah, a buddy of mine is co-owner in this little endeavor, so of course I agreed to come out and support him." His arm was slung over Alexa's chair, stroking her shoulder as he glanced around the room. I was so happy my best friend found love. She certainly deserved her happily ever after. But sometimes her happiness drove home what I'd lost.

Plus, I forever felt like a third wheel, even though both of them assured me it wasn't the case. I knew they were concerned about me, but I declined most of their invitations because I not only wanted to be alone, but I also wanted to give them some time together. I knew, as much as anyone, how important the first stages of a new relationship were. Getting to know each other, even learning how to deal with the stubborn parts of the other person's personalities were obstacles best done alone.

And those two sure had their work cut out for them. Braden was a kind man, but he was pretty intense, sometimes acting as if his word was law. Alexa was stubborn in her own right, sticking to her guns each time he was acting like an ass. Yeah, they definitely had their trying times to deal with but they seemed to really care about one another, despite all of the other noise.

"Well, it's a great place. Your friend should be proud of his accomplishment," I offered.

"Speak of the devil and he shall appear. Here comes the man of the hour now." I wasn't paying attention until Braden stood from his seat, walked away from our table and shook hands with someone. When he moved out of the way and I'd gotten a glimpse of who he was talking to, I'd felt as if I'd been sucker-punched in the gut.

My eyes were as big as saucers, but they were nothing compared to how far wide my mouth had fallen.

Kael was staring right at me as he approached our table. *What the hell?* How does Braden know him? The next thought in my head, of course, was if Alek was there, as well. I knew what good friends they were so I wouldn't be surprised to see him, even though it was the last thing I wanted.

"Sara, how are you?" Kael politely asked.

"Fine, thank you. And you?" I fidgeted in my chair, glancing around everywhere to see if *he* was there.

In the midst of my roving eyes, I landed on Alexa's face, which was one of pure confusion. She leaned over the table, curiosity getting the better of her. "How do you know Braden's friend?" she whispered.

I wasn't sure if I could answer her while holding back the rush of emotion which was sure to spill over. Trying to calm myself, I was able to finally give her something. "Kael is good friends with Alek." I blew out a nervous breath so loud, I was surprised no one at the table made a comment.

"Oh," was all she could say, obviously realizing the same thing I did just moments before. The enormity of the situation wasn't lost on either one of us.

Once the introductions were finished, Kael asked to speak to me in private.

He started first, mainly because I didn't even know what to say. "How are you doing, Sara? Really?" Such a loaded question. One I wasn't comfortable answering. His loyalty fell to Alek and the last thing I wanted to do was put him in an awkward position, finding himself on the side of defending his asshole of a friend. But he *was* going out of his way to talk to me, so the least I could do was give him a truthful answer. *Maybe I'll leave the name-calling for another time.*

"Honestly?" He nodded. "I've been better." It was all I was comfortable saying right then. My curt response said enough. I wanted so badly to ask him if Alek was going to be there, but I didn't want him to think I was still hung up on him. Not knowing what guys talked about, I worried he would run back and tell him everything I said.

"I told him he was making the biggest mistake ever letting you go, but he didn't want to listen to me." He looked a little uncomfortable, but he started it, so I was going to finish it. Plus, it would be nice to release some of my anger onto someone other than poor Alexa.

"Well, I'm sure Cora was only too pleased he broke it off with me." Saying her name was torture on my tongue, acid to my ears.

"Cora? His ex-fiancée? What does she have to do with any of this?" The look of confusion on his face was priceless. His good pal obviously didn't tell him everything.

"She was at his house the night he broke up with me. Well, he didn't actually say the words. No, he wasn't man enough. He simply stood there, not saying a damn thing. I left and never heard from him again. Well, up until a week ago when he apologized but not saying exactly what for. Thankfully, I was able leave before he humiliated me with more lies."

Kael still looked confused, not quite sure what he should and shouldn't say to me. I understood, guy code and all that. He didn't want to overstep, but at the same time he looked like he wanted to offer me some comfort, a small slice of revelation and relief.

"He's not back with Cora, so I'm not even sure what all that was about, Sara." He glanced around, making sure there was no one else nearby to hear our private conversation. "He broke it off with you because the sheer guilt about the things which have happened to you while he was in your life, up-close and personal, were too much to bear. He thought by letting you go, he could better protect you. Like he did before he met you." Before I could even comprehend the impact of his words, he blurted out, "That's why you guys are no longer together. I tried to talk him out of it numerous times, mostly when he was slumped over his couch, drunk as a skunk. He's not doing well, Sara, and if he sees you here tonight, I fear something bad will happen."

Was he telling me the truth? What reason would he have to lie to me? But more than anything, the one comment I chose to focus on was *He's not doing well, Sara, and if he sees you here tonight, I fear something bad will happen.* "Well, I'm not going anywhere, Kael. I don't owe him a damn thing, so I couldn't give a rat's ass if he's pissed I'm here. What's he going to do? Throw me out? He doesn't own this place, you do."

"Well..." *Oh, no. Please, don't say it. Please, don't let what I think he's going to say leave his mouth.* "He's the other owner of Verdana, so he can do whatever he wants." Before I panicked, he calmed me down by putting my mind at ease. Well, kind of. "He's not going to kick you out, Sara. That's not what I meant. I meant, once he knows you're here, he's probably going to drink too much and do or say something stupid. But it's not anything I can't handle. God knows I've had enough practice over the past few months."

He reached out and touched my arm, giving me a half-smile to let me know he realized what an ass his friend was, but all the while being compassionate to the situation. *Why was Kael always the one telling me the important info? First, about Alek having been engaged before and now, the reason why he pushed me out of his life.*

"I have to return to my table." Our conversation was over. I saw no need to drag it out any further.

"Sure thing." He huffed out a quick breath, fidgeting a little before speaking again. "I'll do my best to keep you two apart from each other so tonight goes off without a hitch."

"Thanks, Kael. Really, thank you. For everything. I know Alek is your friend, and I appreciate the kindness you've shown me. It means more than you'll ever know." And it really did. He was a good man. Adara was a lucky woman. Then it hit me. I couldn't believe I hadn't thought about her before. "Is Adara going to be here tonight, as well?" I was hoping for a familiar face, someone who would no doubt take my side.

"She'll be here but not until later. I'll be sure to tell her to find you if you guys are still here."

"Okay. Thanks again." I turned and walked back toward our table, my energy level fully depleted. Once I sat down, Alexa was all over me, desperate to find out what happened.

"Are you okay? Is there going to be a problem? Should we leave?" She was so anxious, not wanting to expose me to another situation so soon after our last encounter.

"No. Everything is fine. I'm okay and we're not going anywhere. I'm not going to let him run me out of here." She had no idea what I was talking about. The only thing she knew was that Alek was friends with Kael, who also happened to be Braden's friend. She didn't know Alek was co-owner, as well. And I wasn't about to tell her right then because she would insist we leave. Braden would no doubt agree with her.

No, I wasn't going anywhere. If he didn't want to see me then he would have to avoid me. He'd had enough practice so far.

Once we settled back into our conversation, we were once again interrupted. But that time it was from Braden's colleague, James, who had just arrived. He took the empty seat next to me, smiling as we shook hands. It was easy to return his enthusiasm because he was quite easy on the eyes. I wasn't typically attracted to blonds, but I made an exception for him. He was quite handsome in his designer suit, hair just so and a sexy smile which certainly turned many heads. He was no Alek, no man was, but he would be the perfect distraction for the evening.

"So, Sara, tell me, what do you do for a living?" He seemed genuinely interested in what I had to say, so I indulged him.

"I own a little flower shop."

"Don't be so modest," Alexa interrupted. "Her shop's so busy she's probably going to have to expand soon." She winked, smiling at my sudden shyness.

James jumped back into the conversation, smiling at me to ease my trepidation some. "I like flowers." I don't know why but his statement made me laugh, and apparently it had the same effect on the rest of the table because they soon joined in. "What? I do," he retorted.

I laughed harder. "I'm sure you do, James. That's not why I'm laughing. It's the way you said it, all eager to compliment what I do for a living. It's sweet. Really, it is."

"Well, then we're off to a good start," he replied, resting his arm on the back of my chair, quickly brushing my shoulder with his finger as he settled in. I froze for a second then mentally berated myself for being too reserved. There was nothing wrong with enjoying myself, which included letting a handsome man flirt with me. I wasn't going to go home with him, so what was the harm?

From the outside, it looked as if I was truly having fun, but the fact was I was still miserable on the inside. Yes, I smiled at the numerous tales being passed around from person to person, laughing when appropriate, but I was numb inside, not really letting the fun of the evening bleed through. All of my thoughts were of Alek and whether or not I was going to lay eyes on him soon. I tried, I really did. I wanted to like James. I wanted to be open to the good times the night was trying to bring, but I couldn't. I couldn't do any of it.

I excused myself, needing to buy another drink to help with the sadness eating me up from the inside. As I approached the bar, my heart stopped. At the far end was the one man I'd been looking for all evening but secretly hoped wouldn't show up.

He was leaning against the bar, laughing with some of the people surrounding him. Kael was there, too, and when I caught his eye, he shifted, no doubt trying to block Alek's view of me. But he overdid it because he ended up bumping into Alek, pushing his arm and knocking over some of his drink. I saw Alek say something to his friend, looking confused for a second before his eyes darted around the room, taking in all of his immediate surroundings.

Then he locked eyes with me.

And I froze like a deer in headlights. I knew I didn't have the strength to confront him again. So what did I do? I hurried back to our table, forgetting all about my liquid courage, and took my seat next to James. I was so afraid to look up, only glancing over at Alexa trying to garner her attention with Morse code, rapidly blinking like some sort of crazy woman.

Then I heard a gasp. It was Alexa.

"Sara. He's coming over here," she mumbled, trying her best to keep her voice down. Before I could react, he was standing by our table.

"How are you folks enjoying your evening?" Alek asked our group. He was standing right next to me, his thigh almost touching my arm. I could smell him. I was innately drawn to him whenever he was near.

I raised my head and stared at Alexa again, my breaths coming in shorter, more rapid succession. Then I glanced over at Braden, and I saw the moment the recognition hit him. He remembered Alek from the bar, no doubt wondering what the hell he was doing at the restaurant opening.

"Fine," Alexa said curtly.

Before anything escalated, Kael appeared out of nowhere to save us. To save me. He stood next to Alek and gripped his shoulder, silently warning him not to cause a scene. When I finally dared to look up at him, I could see his jaw was already ticking, glancing from James to me then back to James again. Well, clearly he knew Braden wasn't with me, but I was sure he was wondering about the man sitting next to me. Because James was oblivious, he reached out and grabbed my hand, and I let him, partly because I was too wrapped up in the intense moment to move, but partly because I wanted Alek to see me with someone else. To realize who he threw away.

Kael broke the uncomfortable silence first. "Braden, this is the other co-owner of the restaurant. Alek Devera. Alek, this is Braden, the guy I was telling you about." They politely nodded at each other, never extending their hand for a hello.

"We've met," Braden said. *Short and sweet.*

The air around our table bristled with tension. The only thing I could think of was to escape and draw away the one person who was causing the issues.

"I'll be right back." I stood up, prompting James and Braden to rise from their seats, as well. I wasn't ten steps away from the table before I could sense Alek following behind me. Resting my hands on the edge of the bar, it was mere seconds before his warm breath cascaded over my neck. But I never turned around. I wasn't strong enough to fight him off again.

"Sara, we need to talk." His hand was against my side.

"We don't have anything to talk about. Please, leave me alone."

He didn't. "Did you know I would be here tonight?" he asked, sounding hopeful. "Is that why you came? Were you hoping to see me?" I didn't have to face him to know he had a smirk on his face, goading me into a conversation.

What an arrogant ass. He really knew how to push my buttons. I stayed strong, however. I fought every instinct I had not to turn around and smash my lips against his.

"Can you please leave me alone, Alek?" I asked him again.

"Answer me first. Were you hoping to see me tonight, Sara?"

"No," I whispered while keeping my head down.

He shifted behind me. Then he grabbed my waist, squeezing me to get my attention.

I'd had enough of his little games. He tossed me aside like yesterday's garbage, for whatever reason, and didn't contact me for three months, then ran into me twice in one week. Trying to persuade me to talk to him like I owed him something. *It's not enough he devastated me twice already, but he wants to do it again?*

No, I won't allow him to hurt me anymore.

I flipped my body around and faced him head-on. We were so close our breaths mingled, our lips temptingly close.

"Baby, please talk to me. I can't take it anymore."

" *You* can't take it anymore? *You?*" I yelled a little louder than I'd intended. Thankfully, I captured Kael's attention, who was on his way over. Hopefully to intercede and not just be a bystander to the war which was undoubtedly going to erupt between the two of us if we continued our little charade.

"Please, can't we go somewhere and talk?" Alek persisted. His teeth captured his bottom lip, chewing on it in his uneasiness.

Kael strode up behind Alek and calmed the volcano before it erupted. That volcano was me. I was about to go off on him and cause a scene because I was on the verge of a breakdown.

He seized Alek by his shoulders and tried to pull him away. "Come on, man. Let's go. Don't do this here." When Alek didn't budge, he gripped him tighter.

"Fine!" he yelled. What the hell was he so angry about? The only person who had any right to be upset was me. The two men walked away, never looking back in my direction. I saw Kael lead him toward the back of the restaurant, disappearing around a corner and out of sight. The next thing I knew, Alexa was standing beside me, doing her best to make sure I was okay. If you didn't know the whole situation, it would have looked like we were all simply having a conversation. But Alexa knew every little detail of our drama, so she was right there to offer her support. Yet again.

"I want to go home, Lex." I closed my eyes to hold back the tears. The last thing I wanted to do was break down in the middle of the restaurant.

"Don't let him win, Sara. Don't let him force you out of here. Normally, I would agree with you and take you home myself, but you're going to have to get used to running into him. And as much as you won't like it, you have to be able to deal with him and not let him dictate where you'll be or for how long. Don't let him have that control over you. Don't give in. Don't let him win, Sara," she repeated.

As much as I wanted to argue with her, I knew she was right. I couldn't let him command anything in my life anymore. With that realization came an unwavering resolve to toughen up, if only for one night. When the bartender finally refilled my drink, we made our way back to the table, our arms linked in unison.

The next hour flew by in a blur. I tried my absolute hardest to ignore Alek, but he was staring at me from across the room.

Because I wanted to goad him, I shamelessly flirted with James by touching his arm and allowing him to grab my hand whenever he wanted.

At one point, I thought Alek was going to run at him, but he didn't. Then I saw the reason he restrained himself.

It was Kael, talking in his ear the entire time.

~25~

Alek

I couldn't take my eyes off her. Being unable to think straight around her had become my new normal. So conflicted with guilt and pain, I failed to tell her why I'd initially pushed her away. Needing to explain myself drove me to invade her space. She was stubborn, though, and I knew she wouldn't hear me out unless I found a way to force her to listen to me.

When I'd made the decision to back away from her, I thought it was the best choice, the responsible choice...for her. But it was killing both of us—me more than her, I thought. She had obviously moved on, not having a care in the world as to whether or not she flaunted another man in my face. Who was he? Was it serious? At first, I thought she was involved with that Braden guy, but I came to find out he was with Alexa.

I was relieved at first, until I learned there was someone new I had to worry about. Well, he wasn't really competition for me. If I could garner her attention, entice her to come over and talk to me, if I could show her there was still an undying connection pulsing between us, I think she would be game for giving us another chance.

Was I being delusional? Probably.

Did I care? Not really.

The question was how could I draw her away from her table? If I approached her again, Kael was going to no doubt punch me. Not that I was afraid of him, but causing a scene was the last thing we needed on opening night. I wasn't that much of a dick, no matter how much pain I was in.

"Hi there," the redhead next to me purred. I was so focused on my agenda I hadn't even realized anyone was next to me. She rubbed my arm, trying to draw my attention.

I was nothing if not polite. "Hi." My greeting was simple but curt. I smiled but didn't want to lead her on. Moving my arm away from her, I signaled to the bartender. When I happened to look down at the other end of the bar, I saw Sara. She was leering at me.

She was pissed, a scowl making her lips turn down in disgust. What was she upset about? I was leaving her alone like she asked.

The woman next to me didn't catch on to my subtle hint, instead placing her hand back on my arm. As soon as she made contact, I witnessed the sour expression on Sara's face again. A lightbulb went off. She was angry some other woman was flirting with me, and she thought I was flirting back.

Looks like I found my new ammunition. The thing I found funny was the fact she thought it was okay to allow some guy to paw at her but the first time she saw another woman vying for my attention, she didn't like it.

I hated playing games, but I found they were my only option available.

I turned my head toward my neighbor and gave her my full attention. Flashing her the Devera, panty-dropping smile, I acted as if I was interested in her advances. I said something witty, making her throw her head back and laugh. She was rather quite beautiful—no comparison to Sara, but a delight on the eyes nonetheless.

After ten minutes of us flirting back and forth and having Sara witness the whole thing, I moved in for the kill.

"What's your name, sweetheart?" I leaned in close, whispering my question in her ear. The whole time I crowded the woman, I was searching for Sara. Our eyes locked, and she was seething. She slammed her drink on the counter and started walking in my direction.

It's working. She's coming over. My heart hammered against my chest, my cock hardening in anticipation for whatever she chose to do or say.

"Tina."

"What?"

"You asked me what my name was. It's Tina," she offered.

Oh, yeah, I did just ask her name. I tried my hardest to keep my attention on Tina, but I saw Sara approaching and I became more excited. She was so close. Only a few more feet and she'd be standing right next to me. When I'd thought she was going to stop and say something, anything, she walked right on by. But not before calling me a dick as she passed.

I couldn't help it. I laughed. I was happy to evoke any kind of reaction from her, even if it was anger. Any emotion meant she still cared, and I wasn't going to let the opportunity pass me by. Enough was enough already. I had to fix us, and there was no time like the present.

"Will you excuse me please, Tara?"

Her smile faltered from my dismissal. "It's Tina."

"Sorry," I apologized, heading toward the women's restroom.

I had to be careful on how I approached her. I had to let her know I was sorry for everything, and I wanted to try and work it out. I thought I made the right decision by backing away from her, from us. But clearly, I chose wrong. I figured the pain would eventually go away, that my love for her would weaken, but it didn't. Both the anguish of our separation and my love for her were growing stronger as time passed, not weaker.

Pushing open the door to the restroom, I didn't see anyone at first. I leaned against the counter, clearly noticing there was only one stall in use. It had to be her. *Please, let her be in there.* If not, I was going to be a tad embarrassed.

A couple of minutes passed before I heard what sounded like crying. Maybe my ears were playing tricks on me. *Why would she be crying? She was pissed not five minutes ago.* The stall door opened and out stepped the woman who was going to be the death of me if I didn't find a way to resolve our predicament.

"Alek? What the hell are you doing in here?" Once I realized we were truly alone, I reached behind me and locked the door. Her eyes followed my hand and widened at the brazenness of my presumption. It was with my bold move I realized the only way to break through her cold exterior toward me was for me to have my hands on her. All over her, to be exact.

"We need to talk. And since you won't listen to me otherwise, I'm locking us in here until you hear what I have to say."

"Of course you are. Because everything has to be on your terms. Nothing's changed, has it?" She flipped on the faucet and washed her hands. Grabbing a paper towel, she did everything she could to avert her eyes from me. "Well, it's not going to work. I have nothing to say to you. So why don't you go back out there and put your charms to good use on the skank at the bar." There was no denying the venom in her voice, and it made me happy. She still felt something for me; she couldn't deny it no matter how much she tried.

"I'm not interested in her." I took a step closer. "I only want you." I took another step in her direction, forcing her to look up at me.

"Since when?" she barked. "Since when do you want me, Alek? Because you've made it very clear the opposite is true." She backed up when I took another step forward, forcing her against the edge of the vanity. "What happened to Cora? Couldn't convince her to stick around?"

The simple mention of her name instantly put me on guard. I hated that she hurt Sara with her confrontation and lies, but at the time, it seemed the best way to push Sara away, to make her angry with me, thinking I was leaving her for my ex-fiancée. Obviously, it was the wrong path to take. I had to tell her the truth.

"I never had any intention of getting back with her. She showed up out of the blue. You have to believe I had no idea she would show up at my house or that she ever had a conversation with you. She didn't tell me about it until after you left."

"I don't believe anything you say to me. Once upon a time, I did. But not anymore." Her body betrayed her words, her heaving chest playing a different tune than what she was saying. Nervously, her tongue wet her bottom lip and it drove me insane. All I wanted to do was bite it, begging for entrance to taste her one more time.

It's now or never.

I was quick. I pinned her against the counter so she couldn't move. My mouth was on hers before she could even protest. Trying to push me away, she struck my chest with her fists, but I didn't budge.

I couldn't back away.

I had to make it right again.

"Please forgive me, Sara," I said, breaking our connection for a brief moment. "I thought I was making the right choice to keep you safe." Never giving any indication she heard my pleas, she continued to fight me. I had no choice but to grab her flailing hands and pin them behind her back, forcing her breasts to jut out with the re-positioning of her arms.

"Get off me. I don't want you, Alek. Let me go." She was so angry with me but I knew if I was able to convince her to be with me, to have her crave our connection again, she would change her mind. But I wouldn't force her. She had to want it as much as I did. It didn't mean I'd release her hands, though; it simply meant I had to seduce her into submission.

"I know you want me deep inside you, baby. Please, let it happen. Let me show you how much I've missed you," I whispered in her ear, nipping at her lobe before I ran my tongue down the side of her lovely throat.

Her only response was to throw her head to the side, exposing more of her neck to me. I smiled. It was a start.

I moved in closer, pressing my cock against her belly, trying to find some sort of comfort, but the only thing I found was frustration. When she felt me against her, she wriggled, a moan escaping her luscious lips. I released her wrists while still lavishing her neck with my mouth, nipping and sucking as if I couldn't get enough. My goal was to place her on top of the vanity, a perfect position for me to slide inside her.

But my trust she would give in faltered when she reached out and slapped me. It came out of nowhere. The look of surprise on my face was telling. I never saw it coming, not even for a second.

I knew I'd hurt her so badly, and if she needed to strike out at me to help release some of her pain then I would gladly allow her to do so. I took a step back, resting my hands at my sides and nodding in understanding.

She struck me again, the sting from her slap settling into my skin like the punishment I deserved. My jaw tightened and my nostrils flared, but I would stand there and take as much as she had to give me.

Preparing for more of her hurt to lash out at me, I was stunned to find she was finished. Her face was expressionless, the only indication she was hurting was the buildup of tears in her eyes. Hitting me again was a much better choice than having to witness her tears. Physical pain I could deal with; it was the emotional pain that tore me up inside.

"I'm so sorry for hurting you, baby. More than you'll ever know."

One tear escaped and slid down her cheek. She was gripping the edge of the vanity so tight her hands were turning white.

I dared to move in closer still, nuzzling my head into her neck. Inhaling her sweet scent almost undid any amount of sanity I was holding onto.

"Please, forgive me." I kissed her throat. "If you give me one more chance, I promise I'll never disappoint you ever again. I swear on my life. Please." I rained kisses all along her jaw, slowly inching closer to her mouth. "I love you, Sara. I thought it was the right choice. I now know what a huge mistake it was." I nipped at her bottom lip, running my tongue over the slight sting. "I can't breathe without you."

More tears escaped as she stared at me. Brushing my thumbs across her cheeks, I did my best to wipe them away. Each one sliced through my heart. I vowed right then and there to never make her cry ever again.

Resting my lips over hers, I waited for her to make the next move. It took her a minute, but she pushed her lips to mine, all the while still holding steady to the marble vanity. I was beyond thrilled she'd finally allowed herself to react to me, in a good way.

I claimed her mouth nice and slow, teasing her as my tongue savored her. We provoked each other for what felt like forever. In reality, it was but a few minutes.

The woman standing in front of me drove me out of my mind. Thankfully, I knew I was going to enjoy the ride.

~26~

Sara

I tried my best to hold on to the last shred of my control. But it was wavering, slowly dissipating with each passing second. I didn't want him. To be more accurate, I didn't *want* to want him. Being next to him, having him invade my personal space, hands touching me, mouth claiming me, he was making me feel again. I wanted to stay numb. It was so much easier to function, to go through the mundane parts of everyday life, if I remained emotionless.

His pleas tore me apart. I knew he was sincere when he spoke and I wanted to forgive him. I really did. But he'd hurt me so badly, I knew it was going to take more than a simple *I'm sorry* and a few minutes of enrapture to convince me to give him another chance.

He'd finally broken the kiss and I didn't press any further. I wanted to see what he was going to do next. What I should've done was push him away and walk right on out of there, but I didn't. I couldn't find the strength to walk away from him again. Not until there was some sort of resolution, or at the very least a promise to...to what? I didn't even know. I was so confused. He knew what he was doing by locking us in the ladies room together. Alone. Where he could break me down with something as simple as his touch.

"Sara," he said, gripping my waist as he pulled me into him. "Please give me another chance. I swear you won't be disappointed."

His tongue slipped from his mouth to wet his bottom lip. I didn't think he even knew what he was doing to me with that one simple action. My eyes were fixated on his mouth. I loved the taste of him. Hungry for more, I tilted my chin up so his mouth hovered over mine but he never moved, which was surprising. Believing he was letting me lead, I trusted he wouldn't push me too far. Not before I was ready.

He pulled back, and the look he gave me held such intensity I almost forgot why I was ever angry with him.

Almost.

"Do you want this?" he asked, hands moving around to my lower back, sliding down and cupping my cheeks as he slowly grinded against me. "Do you want me?" The regret in his eyes told me everything I wanted to know. He was truly sorry for hurting me, and I believed he would never do it again.

I never directly answered his questions, instead telling him something I wanted to say a week before but never did. "I missed you," I whispered, placing my lips back against his.

A groan fell from his mouth as he kissed me again, this time with an undeniable fervor. His hands slid underneath my dress, his fingers teasing my inner thighs until I widened my stance, allowing him the access he needed.

I was done with hurting.

I was done with the numbness.

I was done with denying myself the smallest bit of pleasure.

I gave in to him.

To us.

Grabbing my waist, he hoisted me onto the vanity, hiking my dress up so I was exposed. Palming me over my panties, he teased me until I became slick with arousal. Shifting the lace material to the side, he pushed a finger between my swollen folds but didn't go further. He was allowing me to lead. I would give him consent when I was ready. Little did he know he wouldn't have to wait long at all.

"Please," I begged, running my hands through his hair and pulling him closer. "Alek, please." My begging broke him. He thrust two fingers deep inside me, wasting no time by curving his fingers to rub against the sweet spot he knew would drive me crazy.

"Goddamn it, Sara," he moaned. "I can't take much more." He cradled his head into the crook of my neck. "Please, tell me I can have you. Please, tell me you're not going to torture me and make me wait to claim what's mine." His free hand moved up my body and pulled down the top of my dress. With the skill only he possessed, he freed my breast and teased me first with his fingers then with his glorious mouth.

It was too much. Everything hit me like a tidal wave all at once. The hurt and despair etched into my very existence, all came crashing down on me. Then there was the pleasure, overshadowing anything I'd felt over the past three months. Seeing Alek again was almost surreal. I never thought I would lay eyes on him ever again, and there he was, looking for me at the bar a week ago.

Then I walked into the same restaurant he owned with Kael. What the hell were the chances?

I was thrown from my thoughts when the familiar pull coiled in my belly. His thumb was stroking my clit as his fingers thrust inside me. "Fuuuuuuck," I moaned. "Faster. Do it faster." There was no time for shame or shyness. I had one goal in mind, and I was going to claim it no matter what.

He strummed me faster, giving me exactly what I cried for. Gripping his shoulders, I spread my legs wider and pumped against his hand. My walls tightened and he knew what was happening. He barely latched onto my mouth to swallow my screams as I came. He never let up, simply slowing down his movements as my orgasm subsided.

"I want you to take me, Alek," I demanded, reaching down and unhooking his belt from his pants.

"I can't believe I'm going to ask you this, but...are you sure?" He smiled, but there was no denying the serious tone to his question.

"Yes, I am."

I was tired of overthinking everything.

I wanted him to move inside me.

I wanted him to continue to devour me with his kiss.

I wanted to be his very lifeline, his only breath.

Moving my hands away, he ripped off his belt, unhooked the button and slid his zipper down. Pushing his pants and boxer briefs down his thighs, I was left with the sight of his thick cock in his hand. It always excited me and I made a mental note to demand he pleasure himself in front of me, exactly like what I'd done for him.

"Are you all right? You seem overly flushed." His brow arched as he drank in my wanton state.

"You know damn well what you do to me. Now, will you please ravage me?" I tempted.

"Well, when you ask like that..."

Leaning back on the vanity, I raised my legs so my feet were resting on the edge as well, fully exposed and ready for him to do whatever he wanted. He lowered himself until his face hovered over my slick need. One swipe of his tongue and I was a goner. To add to his sweet torture, his thumb lightly grazed my clit, the smallest touch setting off fireworks. He continued to rub my sensitive bundle of nerves, his mouth closing over me until I was set to explode. Soft mewls escaped me as he continued to work my body.

The image of his head buried between my thighs was enough to make me combust but before I even found my rhythm, he retreated.

Hoisting me up, he lowered me back down, never taking his hands from me until my feet were firmly on the ground.

Looking perplexed, I asked, "What are you doing?" Without answering, he gently turned me around to face the mirror.

"I want you to watch yourself as you come all over me, Sara." Flipping back up my dress, he pushed me forward so I was bracing myself on the counter. I heard the noise from the condom wrapper before he positioned himself at my entrance. I looked up into the mirror and his eyes instantly found mine. He smiled as he slid inside me, inch by inch, until he was in so deep he pressed against my womb.

At first he moved slow, relishing finally being able to take me again after so long. But the more time passed, the more his grip on my waist tightened. "You're so beautiful," he whispered, leaning his head into the side of my neck. His breath tickled my skin, his kisses driving me beyond the brink. "Look at me, baby. Look at what you do to me."

My eyes fixated on our reflection and what I saw was my absolute undoing. His eyes were laced with desire, his teeth clenched in anticipation of our unraveling. Together.

His gyrations stroked the simmering burn, tightness curling its way down my belly and unfolding at the apex of my thighs.

He knew I was close.

He knew the changes in my breathing when I was right on the edge.

"Alek...I'm there," I panted. "I'm right there." My grip on the counter intensified, allowing me to meet his every thrust.

Our dance was perfect.

With each stroke, he managed to tear down another piece of my fortress, an invisible structure I'd built to protect my heart.

During the height of our joining, I'd absently closed my eyes. Resting his hands on my throat, he whispered in my ear, "Look how beautiful you are, baby." Once I'd locked eyes on him again, on us, I willfully dove off the cliff, free-falling into the pleasurable abyss he was raining all over my body.

"Fuck!" he panted. "I can't hold out anymore." With a few more punishing drives, he shouted out his own release. His forehead rested between my shoulders. Clearly he was spent, but I never stopped moving. I wanted to slowly milk every last bit of his pleasure. "If you don't stop, I'm going to be ready to go again in two minutes."

"Two minutes? Really? That long?" I teased.

"That's not long, considering I'm still not done coming inside you."
Wow!

Once he'd finally slipped from my body, something changed. I hadn't regretted what we'd done, but a wave of unexpected emotions washed over me. I needed time. Time by myself to sort through everything and make sure I was making the right decision by giving him a second chance. *Or should I say third chance?*

Fixing my dress, I disappeared into the nearest stall to clean myself up before going back out into the restaurant. Surely, Alexa was wondering what had happened to me. Although I'd only been gone twenty minutes, it was enough of an absence to garner questioning.

As I washed my hands, I made sure to avoid looking at him. If I made eye contact or touched him in any way, I would throw all caution to the wind and take him back without question. Although it was a path I was almost certain I was going to take, I needed some time to be certain.

"I have to go, Alek."

He moved closer, reaching out to try and pull me into him. When I moved back, the look on his face almost killed me. He thought I was slipping away again, and it almost crushed him.

"Why are you pulling away from me, Sara? I told you how sorry I was. I meant it," he pleaded. "I'll do anything you need. Just tell me. Please."

I was going to release his worry right then but I decided to let him wallow in a little bit of doubt. For a while. He deserved it after what he put me through.

"Give me the night to sort through everything." They were my parting words to him. As I brushed past him on my way to the door, our hands touched, sending a bolt of electricity through both of us.

There was no way I'd ever be able to break the hold which locked us together. I knew it, and so did he. A slight smile graced his mouth as I disappeared from his sight.

Rushing toward our table, all eyes were locked on me as I approached, and guilt swirled up inside me. "Are you okay, Sara?" James asked as he stood to pull out my chair. But I wasn't staying.

"I'm not feeling too well." I looked first at my date, giving him a slight smile before locking eyes with Alexa. "Can you give me a ride home, please?"

"Of course." There was no hesitation on her part as she leaned over and whispered something in Braden's ear before grabbing her things and ushering me out the door.

I filled her in on everything, from my little talk with Kael to having sex with Alek in the ladies room. To say she was shocked was an understatement, but as she made her way to our apartment, she smiled, knowing her best friend was coming back to her.

As I laid my head on my pillow and drifted off to sleep, I couldn't help but wonder what the following day would bring.

~27~

Alek

What the hell happened? One second, I was buried in her sweet body and the next, she ran from me. I thought we were making progress, yet she said she needed the night to think things over.

Sara liked to overthink, and it could mean the difference between me living again or wasting away without the love of my life next to me. I wouldn't push her, though. As hard as it was, I was going to give her the time she needed. But rest assured, I'd be on her doorstep come early-morning light.

I cleaned myself up and gathered whatever was left of my composure before exiting the bathroom. As soon as I walked out, Kael was standing directly in front of me, blocking my path to the bar.

Maybe I should give the alcohol a rest.

"What did you do to her?" he hissed, clutching my shirt in his fists. "She rushed out of here so fast, as if someone had done something to her," he repeated slowly.

I shoved him away from me, straightening myself before answering. "I didn't do anything to her. Well..." I smirked, but apparently it was the wrong move.

"So help me, God, Alek." My dear friend was more worried about Sara than he was about me. I liked it. He knew how to keep me in check, and I appreciated him even more for it. "Don't hurt her again."

"I'm not going to. I promise. Things happened between us," I said, subconsciously rubbing my palm over the front of my pants, "and I think she's coming around." My eyes lit up for the first time in months, and nothing Kael could say would diminish it.

Settling in at the bar, I ordered a club soda. I knew we still had hours to go before closing up and I needed to give our restaurant's opening some much needed attention. Leaving everything to my friend and partner was a shitty move, but I was there and I was finally ready to deal with whatever he needed from me.

I'd noticed Braden and the guy who was sitting next to Sara were still at their table. Thankfully, they didn't stay too much longer, paying their bill and disappearing twenty minutes later. I knew Alexa had been the one to take Sara home because she was missing, plus those two were like sisters. Alexa would never let her leave alone.

An hour before closing, an unwelcome sight walked through the door, throwing me into an instant fit of rage.

Cameron.

I'd been planning on paying him a visit but I never found the time, what with me being mostly drunk over the past few months.

He never saw me approach, too busy chatting up the unsuspecting female bartender. I quickly snatched him by the neck and dragged him outside into the alleyway next to the building before he even knew what was happening. His reaction was slow, and once I turned him to face me, I realized it was because he was on something. He wasn't drunk, and he was lucid, but there was a blankness to his stare which told me he'd taken some kind of drug earlier.

"Well, well. If it isn't my favorite cousin," he sneered, pushing me back as his false sense of strength took hold. Cameron was no match for me when we were kids, and he still wasn't as grown men. Because I wasn't in the best of moods, I decided to toy with him a little, taking out any and all of my frustrations on him. He deserved every bit of what I was going to give him. He'd fucked with me, and with Sara, for the last time. Even if Sara hadn't walked into my restaurant that evening, contemplating giving me another chance, I still would have delivered his punishment for his past behavior.

I'd always brushed off my cousin's antics in the past because I'd learned to tolerate him, thinking because he was family I had to. But the older we got, the more I realized I truly despised him. He didn't possess one good quality—none I knew of, at least. Then again, I chose not to interact with him unless I absolutely had to.

The only thing I knew about my dear cousin was that essentially he was alone, never having found anyone to connect with and share his shitty life with. He had money and the Devera looks, but he was an asshole.

Selfish. It was one of the best words to describe him.

I rolled up the cuffs of my sleeves, never saying a word as I tackled him to the ground. Surprise lit up his face as we rolled around together, my fists landing everywhere on his unsuspecting body.

His grunts only fueled me more. "Don't you ever go near Sara again," I bellowed, my fist splitting the side of his lip. "Or I'll kill you. Do you understand me?" I gripped him by the shirt, raised him up and landed another hit to his jaw, throwing his head to the side with the force of my blow.

Something inside me snapped and I took it out on Cameron. Most of it he deserved, but some of it he took because I couldn't control myself.

My fist was pulled back, ready to unleash another wave of anger when all of a sudden, a quick surge of energy pulsed through him and he managed to throw me off him.

Then he attacked.

While his moves were all over the place, effectively from whatever he was on, he managed to catch me in the face. In the eye, to be exact. It hurt like a bitch, and I knew I was going to have one hell of a shiner for sure.

But for every one of the hits he'd been able to land, I returned ten. He was going to look pretty battered and bruised when I was done with him.

We went at it for what felt like forever, but only five minutes had passed since I'd dragged him outside. Thankfully, no patrons were milling around outside the restaurant, so our scuffle was done in private. Or as private as a dark alleyway would allow.

Cameron never said a word while we went at each other. I think he was still in shock I'd actually attacked him. Whatever the reason, his silence was the smartest decision he ever made, because his voice alone would only fuel his beating.

Finally, after I'd expended all the energy I had in me, I staggered to my feet and stepped back. Glaring down at his battered body, I dragged him out of the alleyway and propped him against the far end of the building. It was late, but someone would surely find him. While he was out cold, he was nowhere near death's door. Just a good ol'-fashioned beating was what he'd endured.

Entering the restaurant through the back entrance was a smart decision. I didn't want to listen to Kael lecture me. Plus, we still had customers, and how would it look if one of the owners appeared back inside looking the way I did?

My hair was mussed.

My shirt was splattered with blood.

My knuckles were raw, and my eye was swelling.

Disappearing into my office, I cleaned myself up quickly and changed my clothes. The only evidence I'd been in a fight was from my eye, but it wasn't too bad yet.

How it would look in twenty-four hours would be a different story.

~~~~

I couldn't wait any longer. After giving her the night to think things through, I walked toward her apartment. Waiting longer than I normally would have, I knocked on her door. Pacing back and forth, I prayed she didn't send Alexa out to tell me she didn't want to see me.

We had an unbreakable connection, and I only hoped Sara realized what a rare thing it was. I knew I messed up. Big-time. But I vowed to make it up to her for the rest of my life, if she only gave me the chance to do so.

I wasn't sure what more I could say to convince her how sorry I was for everything I'd put her through. All I knew was I couldn't wait one more second to see her, to breathe her in and hold her in my arms.

I knocked on the door one more time, waiting for my future to greet me on the other side.

~28~

Sara

Soft rapping on the front door tore me from sleep. Looking over at my alarm clock, I saw it was eight in the morning. There was no doubt in my mind who it was. He'd technically given me the night to think things over, so I couldn't be too upset with him.

As I headed toward the front room, thoughts of the previous night bombarded me. To think, the only thing I was nervous about was being set up on a blind date. Never in a million years did I imagine Alek being one of the owners of Verdana, let alone seeing him there then ending up having sex with him in the bathroom. Granted, it was extraordinary, but still one of the biggest shockers of my life thus far.

I took a quick breath as my fingers clutched the handle. Pulling the door open, I was hit with his presence, so powerful and a bit overwhelming. As I looked him over from head to toe, my eyes instantly flew to his face. More specifically to his eye.

Reaching for his hand, I pulled him inside. "What the hell happened to your face?" I asked, rushing toward the freezer to grab an ice pack.

Wrapping the compress in a towel, I walked back over to him and gently pressed it to his face. His hand covered mine as we both held it to his eye. The connection wasn't lost on me, but I pushed it aside for the time being.

I stood in front of him, waiting for him to answer me, my curiosity killing me the longer he remained silent. Finally, he spoke up.

"Cameron." One word and I knew it was pretty bad. The only evidence Alek had was a black eye and a small cut in the corner of his mouth. I could only imagine what his cousin looked like.

"Oh, my God, Alek. What happened?" I asked, ushering him toward the couch to take a seat.

"I don't really want to talk about it." *Wrong answer.* The look on my face said as much. If there was any hope for us, I needed him to tell me everything, even when he didn't want to. "Sorry," he grumbled before he regaled me with the entire story.

I couldn't say I didn't see it coming sooner or later. Relief washed over me I wasn't there to witness it, though. Watching two grown men go toe-to-toe, especially when one of them was Alek, was too much for me to handle.

Taking his hand away from his face, he placed the ice pack on the table beside the couch. Silence fell between us as we continued to stare at each other.

"Sara," he started. "I came here to end our separation. I made a huge mistake, and I fully intend on making things right between us again." Scooting closer, he placed his warm palm on my thigh. "I promise I'll never hurt you again." He looked down at his lap. "Please, forgive me."

I hooked my finger under his chin and coaxed his head to look up. Normally, I was the one averting my eyes from him, not the other way around. Knowing his heart was breaking, the fear in his stare telling me he was afraid I wasn't going to give us another chance was enough for me to move toward him and place my lips against his.

My one small gesture was what he was yearning for. Expelling a quick rush of air, he stood from the couch, reached forward and tangled his hand with mine. Once I was standing in front of him, he pulled me into his embrace, burrowing his face into the crook of my neck. I heard him inhale and knew he was trying to breathe in as much of me as he could, afraid I would back away from him any minute.

"I love you," he whispered in my ear. His body tensed as he waited for me to say something. Anything.

Drawing away from him, I saw his face fall until he heard my words. "I love you, too, Alek. Sometimes more than I want to, but I do."

All fear and reservation floated away from him as he smiled wide and crushed me to him. Peppering kisses all over my face causing me to laugh. "I swear, baby, never again. Never again will I make you cry." He kissed the sensitive spot under my ear. "Never again will I make you doubt my love for you." Gently biting down on my lobe sent a pulse of pleasure straight through me. "Never again will I make you angry."

Still smothered in his embrace, I called him out on his lie. "Now, you know *that* one's not true." We both laughed at his choice of words.

"Okay, how about this? Never again will I purposely make you angry." I furrowed my brow. "Okay, I'll try again. How about I'll do my best to take your thoughts and feelings into consideration before I place any crazy demands on you?" I smiled. "Better?" he asked, still snuggling me into his body.

"Better," I replied.

After hours of *catching up*, we talked late into the evening. He explained in better detail his reasoning for pushing me away, as well as his interaction with Cora and his fight with Cameron. He vowed to never lie to me again and to always come to me first with anything that was bothering him before he made any life-altering decisions.

After listening to everything he had to say, I understood him a little more than I had before. Obviously, some of his decisions were wrong and I made sure to tell him so, to which he simply replied, "I know. I know."

There was a lot we still had to work out, but I finally agreed to give him his third and final chance.

~29~

Sara

Tap. Tap. Tap.

What is that noise? Is it raining?

Still lost in a haze of bliss and sleep, my brain took extra time to catch on to what was going on around me.

Tap. Tap. Tap.

"Hmmmm..." I mumbled, gently stretching out my limbs. Lying on my stomach, I gathered the pillow in my hands as I pressed my face into the soft cloud of goose feather. It took me a little while to realize it wasn't raining at all, that the tapping sound I thought I heard was coming from someone lightly smacking my ass. Over and over again.

Tap. Tap. Tap.

"What?" I whined, wanting nothing more than to fall back asleep.

"Wake up, sleepyhead." *Tap. Tap. Tap.*

The only reason Alek would have to wake me from a sound sleep would be because he was hungry again. For me. Although the thought was tempting, I hadn't been asleep for long, the night's activities surely going into the late hour.

Against my protests, he tried to rouse me again.

"Hmmmmm. What are you doing?" I said in my sleepiest voice.

"Come on, baby, you have to wake up now." Alek's voice was but a whisper, almost as if he was trying not to alarm me, but instead to wake me very slowly.

I twisted my body toward him, still half-asleep. Stretching out, I draped my arm around him, pulling my body so close I was able to wrap my leg around his waist.

He laughed as he kissed my temple.

"Make love to me, Alek," I murmured before clutching him even closer.

"For as much as I would love to, sweetheart, you're going to be late. You have to wake up. Now." His warm breath tickled my ear, making me think naughty thoughts.

Wait...what does he mean I'm going to be late?

I tried to rub myself against him one more time, but surprisingly, he unhitched my leg from his waist and hopped out of bed.

Hmph! Well, if he didn't want to give me some lovin', then I was going back to sleep. I rolled over on my side and closed my eyes, but not before catching a glimpse of the time glaring at me from my alarm clock. My eyes snapped open as I threw the covers off me. Hurrying toward the bathroom, I shouted over my shoulder, "Why didn't you wake me up, Alek?" I never heard his answer as I slammed the door and turned on the water.

Taking the fastest shower known to man, I ran back into my bedroom, threw on some clothes and gathered my hair into a messy bun. The whole while, Alek lazed across my bed, resting on his elbows as he watched me run around like a crazy person. His eyes never left me, the corners of his lips turned up as if he was privy to his own inside joke. "What's so amusing? Do you like seeing me run around like a nut job?"

"No, of course not. It's just I'm the happiest man alive today." There was such sincerity and love laced in his sentiment, it made me stop for a second and take it all in. I never thought I would ever see him again, yet there he was, back in my life. It was all a little surreal. We still had a long road ahead of us, but I was willing to try again.

I sidled up next to him, rested my hands on his thighs and leaned in close to give him a kiss. "I'm going to be late for work."

He followed me outside where we said our goodbyes, making plans for dinner later that evening. A huge smile was plastered on my face as I headed to the shop. I knew I should enjoy every second of it because if life had taught me anything, it was that happiness was fleeting. There was always something unexpected lurking around the corner.

~~~~

I muddled through my normal routine at work, the only difference being I was smiling and laughing more, and apparently people took notice.

"My, my, my. Aren't we in a good mood today?" Megan commented. It'd been over three months since I'd hired her on a temporary basis. She was working out well, so I'd taken her on permanently as a part-time employee. Her personality really jived with not only mine and Matt's, but the other part-timers, as well. She was a good fit.

"What's the occasion?" she asked, looking me over as if the answer was somewhere on my person.

"Let's just say my love life is back to where it should be." I found I was almost giddy with excitement.

"Ohhhh, you met someone," she cooed. Cradling her head in her hands, she leaned forward on the counter. "Tell me all about him. Where did you meet?" Before I could answer, she blurted out, "Wait, is it the guy your friend set you up with last night?" I forgot I even mentioned my plans to her.

"No, not exactly. It's an ex-boyfriend I've re-connected with recently." *Recently as in last night.* "Everything happened so fast, but it's official." I was smiling so big I didn't even notice her face at first.

"Tell me it's not the jerk who came in here the first day I started." Her lip curled up in disgust at the mere thought of him, which instantly put me on the offensive. I think she realized what she'd said because she tried to smooth things over. Well...sort of. "Sorry, I don't like him. He rubs me the wrong way, Sara."

"Well, Megan," I started, reminding myself everyone was entitled to their own opinion, even if it was the opposite of every other red-blooded woman out there who ever came in contact with the man. "Yes, Alek and I are back together. I'm simply curious. Why don't you like him? Was he rude to you or something?"

"Not per se. I don't know. I have a bad feeling about him, that's all."

"Well, I can assure you he's a good man. A bit intense sometimes, but a good man nonetheless."

"If you say so," she mumbled, making her way toward the back of the shop. I wasn't going to let anyone dampen my mood, especially someone who didn't even know him.

Reveling in my own glee for once proved to be an effective tool for making the workday fly by.

~30~

Sara

After dinner, I agreed to accompany Alek back to his house. I hadn't been there since *that* night. Pushing all unpleasant thoughts from my mind, I forged ahead with the continuation of our lovely evening.

"I meant to ask you this at dinner, but I forgot," I purred as he kissed my neck. We were relaxing on his couch in the den when I decided to broach the subject of Megan.

"You did?" he teased, pulling my earlobe gently through his teeth. He couldn't care less what I was trying to ask him, his only concern surely to rid me of my clothes.

The fact my newest employee couldn't stand him was weighing on me more than I thought it would. "What did you ever do to Megan to make her not like you?" I plucked a piece of lint off his sweater as I waited for his response.

"Who's Megan?"

"She's the new girl...you were giving me a hard time about...when you decided to drop by that one day." I couldn't believe he didn't remember. It wasn't as if I hired new people all the time. He shrugged as if he had no idea who I was talking about. "Well, she sure doesn't think much of you at all. You must be losing the old Devera charm," I teased as I playfully tapped his cheek.

"Never." He laughed, digging his fingers into my sides as he tickled me. I fell back on the couch, trying to break his hold, but it was no use. He laid his body over mine and kissed me, his fingers poised to dig in again at the moment of his choosing. "Besides, I don't care what anybody else thinks about me, except you."

"But for her to not like you is weird, don't you think?"

"Well, yeah. But I didn't *do* anything to her, so I can't really say why she's turned off by me." He pushed his arousal into my belly, stopping all conversations about Megan. "Wanna go to bed?"

How could I ever say no to that question?

Alek was not two steps over the threshold of the bedroom before he was stripping off his clothes. He was only a couple of paces in front of me, but it was enough of a head start for him to hop in bed and nestle in.

"Hurry up, baby. I'm getting lonely over here." He flipped the covers back as I turned off the overhead light, licking my lips in anticipation of what was to come. Thankfully, the bedside lamp was still on because I almost tripped over his damn shoes.

Alek insisted there always be some sort of light on while we had sex. He said he loved to watch my body tremble under his touch, and watching my face as he made me come was the sexiest thing he'd ever seen.

Who am I to argue?

After quickly discarding my clothes, I snuggled in close, throwing my leg over his waist and rubbing the neediest part of me against his excitement. I was tracing the lines of his chest when his voice startled me. "You know what? I *do* remember who you're talking about."

"Hmmm..." I panted, kissing his neck and inhaling his intoxicating scent.

"Sara? Did you hear me?" My answer to his question was to straddle his waist, grinding myself on top of him. But for some reason, he wasn't having any of it. He pushed me back so I was sitting upright, his hands on my bare breasts as he held me in place. "Now that you mention it, I still want you to give me her information so I can do my own background check."

Of course, he would pick right then to act like...himself. "Alek, we already discussed this before. I told you then and I'll tell you now...I'm not giving you her information. It's insulting you don't trust I'll do my homework."

"But you don't have the same experience I do when it comes to dealing with shady people, Sara. I know what to look for that you don't." The whole time I was sitting on top of him, his fingers played with my breasts, gently pinching my nipples between his fingers.

"Did you buy a P.I. firm I don't know about?"

"Ha, ha. Very funny." He flipped me onto my back, spreading my thighs with his leg. His fingers danced over my skin, goosebumps popping up the lower he ventured. Kissing my belly, he mumbled, "It would make me feel so much better if you just let me handle this."

Swiveling my hips, I weaved my fingers through his hair as I pushed him lower still. "You're doing perfect," I moaned, "handling...this."

Pressing my thighs wider apart, he tasted me. His tongue lavished me while his lips locked around my clit. Sucking gently, I thrust toward his face as I chased my orgasm. Just as I was on the brink, he pulled back. "What are you doing?" I cried out.

"Please, let me handle this." He sat back on his knees as he ran his finger through my swollen folds.

"I *was* letting you handle it until you stopped. Now please, stop teasing me," I pleaded, squeezing my nipples while he looked on.

"I'm not talking about this, Sara," he said as he palmed me. "I'm talking about letting me do the background check."

"Are you serious right now?" I asked, a little more than baffled he was still trying to convince me to give in.

Refusing to answer the obvious, he pushed two fingers into my tight heat, crooking them until they flicked over my G-spot. My back instantly arched off the bed and I cried in pleasure. "Yes...do it again." He did. His actions were deliberate, partly in hopes I'd allow him to check on my new hire.

"Tell me what I want to hear, sweetheart," he pressed, stroking the sensitive spot over and over. "Come on, tell me."

"I'm so close, Alek." Gripping the sheets, I rotated my hips, trying to garner any additional friction I could to push me over the edge.

"Tell me."

I stopped listening to him, instead focusing on what my body needed right then. "Yes...Yes...Oh, God...I'm coming!" I screamed, my cries tearing from my throat as my entire body shuddered under his touch.

As my heart finally slowed its beating frenzy, my desire for the man in front of me was my only focus. I wanted him to take me fast and hard, to which I knew he wouldn't have a problem.

Extending my arms, I tried to entice him to lie on top of me. Missionary was one of my favorite positions because it allowed me to feel the weight of him as he ravaged my body. I loved the sensation of his skin against mine, being able to clutch onto his arms as his muscles tensed from his exertion.

Instead of covering me with his body, he pulled me up until I was resting on my knees. "Do you want to try something new?" he asked, drawing circles around my nipples with the soft pad of his fingertip.

I wasn't quite sure what he had in mind, but I trusted him. Knowing he wouldn't ask me to do anything I wouldn't like gave me the courage to go along, nodding when he cocked his eyebrow in question.

Spinning me around so I faced away from him, he leaned over and kissed my shoulder. "This isn't new," I said pensively. "We've had sex doggie-style before." As I turned my head to see him, my hair fell in my face, blocking him from view. Pushing the annoying strands out of the way, I was able to finally see his reaction, a mischievous grin plastered all over his face.

"We're not going to fuck doggie-style," he assured me.

Pulling on the drawer of his bedside table, he reached in and grabbed something. I naturally assumed it was a condom, but instead a small bottle was held tight in his grip.

"What is that?" I asked, thoroughly confused.

"Lubrication."

I blew out a breath of relief. He must have bought the wrong box of protection and needed to use something extra to coat it. "Did you pick up the wrong condoms again?" I teased.

"It was one time, and you know damn well I was willing to go without." He laughed, wiggling his eyebrows to make me smile.

"Alek," I tested. "Don't even start, because it's never going to happen."

"Don't say never, baby. In fact, we don't need to use condoms tonight."

"Yeah? And why is that?"

"Because the kind of sex we're going to have will definitely not result in you becoming pregnant."

Having a conversation with him while my ass was in his face was a little awkward. I still didn't understand what he was talking about, though. What kind of sex would never get me pregnant? Why was he holding a bottle of lube in his hand? And why was I on all fours?

Closing my eyes, my head dropped in realization as to what he was essentially asking me to do. It took me a little while to catch on because he'd never even so much as mentioned wanting to have...anal sex.

Alexa had told me once she'd tried it before and really enjoyed it, but only after she got over the initial pain of it.

"You wanna have sex *that* way?" I asked, doing my best to control my nervous breathing.

"I'd like to try it with you, yes." He fisted himself and pressed against me. "I've claimed your mouth." He slowly raked his fingers down my back. "I've claimed your sweet pussy." The tip of his cock pushed against my clit. "Now it's time I claim that luscious ass of yours." Something pressed against my puckered hole and I instantly clenched up.

Slowly, he pushed the tip of his finger inside me. It felt so foreign and...odd.

"You have to relax."

"I'm trying to, but we've never done anything like this before." I swung my head over my shoulder again. I had to see his face when I asked him, "This is going to hurt, isn't it?"

"Yes." *Well, don't sugarcoat it for my benefit.* "At first, but once I'm in, you'll love it. Trust me."

Trust him? On this? He'd obviously forgotten I knew how large he was. He was most likely going to do some damage, but he was trying to convince me I'd love it? All of my paranoia caused me to clench up even more.

"Sara, you're tensing again. Relax, sweetheart."

"I'm trying," I hollered. "But the anticipation of what it's going to feel like is not helping."

"Okay. Well then, how about this?" I waited for him to say something else, but instead he withdrew his finger, and the next thing I felt was his tongue as he licked my pussy. Then he slowly made his way toward the part of me he wished to claim.

I stilled all movement. His touch was faint, at first, but the more he teased me, the more I relaxed. Leaning back into his mouth, I allowed my body to feel, shutting off any and all reservations I had about such an intimate act.

"Alek," I cried out, rocking against his mouth a little faster each time.

"That's it, baby. Do you like that?" His voice was so damn sexy, turning me on even more, if it was even possible.

"I love it," I answered breathlessly.

"Good." He moved off the bed and stood behind me, pulling me back toward the edge until I was positioned where he wanted me.

I heard the click of the bottle as he opened it, then a few seconds later, I heard the same noise as he sealed it shut.

My breathing suddenly picked up pace, nervousness racking my entire body.

Something cold pressed against my virgin area, and before I could say anything, his finger slipped inside once more, that time with a little more ease. The feeling was certainly strange but the more he stretched me, the less it hurt. Until he added a second finger. Tensing up again, I tried to wriggle away but his hold on my waist was firm.

"Sara, you're never going to become used to my touch if you try to move away from me." I knew without even looking at him he was smirking.

"Easy for you to say," I huffed.

He slowed his intrusion until I released some of my anxiety. The more he pumped in and out of me, the more I loosened up, which was quite a relief.

"I'm going to add another finger." His words instantly had me clenching. "Relax, sweetheart," he soothed, leaning forward to kiss my neck. "You're doing so well. You'll be able to take me much easier when I'm done."

After he was finished preparing me, he withdrew his fingers and grabbed my waist.

"Are you ready?" he asked as he pulled me toward him.

I wasn't going to lie. I almost freaked out when he seized my hips and pushed the tip of his cock near my tight entrance. "Please go slow," I pleaded. Maybe I was making more out of it than I should. Maybe I'd end up loving it, like he said.

Maybe...*goddamnit!* He pushed past the exterior, a burning sensation radiating all through me. Squeezing my eyes shut, I tried to breathe through the pain and not focus on the strange feeling of being stretched apart.

There was certainly pain. He hadn't lied about that part.

"That's it, baby. You're doing great. Try and relax some more. Then I'll be able to push in the rest of the way."

"Oh, God, Alek. I think you're going to rip me in two." He was so large the burning sensation was only getting worse. Trying to focus on something...anything else proved to be quite difficult. I was about to tell him I couldn't do it when I felt his finger start to stroke my clit. By re-directing my focus, he'd distracted me enough to relax, essentially decreasing the pain from him pushing further inside me.

The more pleasure his fingers coaxed from me, the more my muscles stretched around him, pulling him in and contracting around the thick steel of his erection.

"I'm in all the way now, but I won't move right away. I want to give you time to adjust to me." His hold on my hips was almost as fierce as his entry. I knew he was on the verge of losing control and he was trying to rein it in until he made me explode. "You're so unbelievably tight, Sara," he groaned. "Luckily, it won't take much for me to come this way." As soon as he moved, I instantly tensed back up. His hand worked me faster, his fingers pinching and rubbing my clit until I couldn't see straight. It was hard to figure out where to focus, the pain or the pleasure. Which one was greater?

"The more I move, the more your muscles will accept me and loosen up, giving you the pleasure I promised." *God, I hope he's right.* The burning had lessened the longer he was deep inside me, but for the life of me, I couldn't imagine it actually being enjoyable.

As he moved again, a tickle of pleasure soon shot through me. "That feels..." I couldn't even find the right words.

"What does it feel like?" he asked, rocking back and forth behind me. Suddenly, my head was pulled back as he captured my hair in his hand. "Fuck me, Sara," he moaned.

Before long, I shouted out something I never thought I would have five minutes earlier. "Harder," I panted. "Alek...please...fuck me a little harder." Intense pressure was building, and I wanted to ride the wave all the way to the end.

"Like that?" he asked, slamming into me with a little more force. "Does that feel good?" He thrust in two more times. Animalistic sounds tore from his throat as he fought not to lose control.

"Yes," I whimpered. My words escaped me. Hell, I could barely breathe from all of the different sensations firing off inside me. I was so close, so near the precipice of release, the only thing I could do was lean down and bite the pillow, pushing my ass higher in the air for him.

Each stroke of his touch, both inside and outside of my body, sent me on a rollercoaster ride of desire, threatening to career off the rails at any second. It was by far the most erotic thing we had ever done.

"I'm gonna come, Sara." He pushed himself in and out with two long strokes. "Come with me." He caressed me with such precision I had no choice but to allow my orgasm to rip through me.

I screamed out my release as he let go of my hair, grasped my hips and chased after his own pleasure.

A short while later, he'd withdrawn from me and immediately asked, "Are you all right? How do you feel?" After his initial desire had lessened, a look of worry shadowed over him.

"I'm fine, Alek," I assured him. "We just won't be doing *that* again for a while."

He chuckled. "Fair enough."

Following his normal after-sex clean-up ritual, he crawled into bed behind me, pulling me into his body so he could hold me tight. Inhaling my scent always relaxed him. I wasn't sure why, but it did.

"Love you, baby," he whispered, quickly fading into sleep.

"Love you, too," I answered, squeezing his hand in mine as I followed him into dreamland.

~31~

Sara

I finally decided to take Megan up on her offer to grab a drink after work. She'd been asking me for months, but I'd been too depressed to even entertain the thought. Normally, I wouldn't go for drinks with an employee, other than Matt, of course, but I liked her. I was her boss above all else, and she knew it, but she was someone I could see having a long-term friendship with.

Alek was already aware I had plans for the evening. He'd tried to persuade me to go to Throttle or even Verdana, but I didn't think it was a good idea. We wanted to go somewhere low-key, somewhere we could sit down and actually hear ourselves think.

He never forced the issue, which was quite an improvement. Curbing his overbearing ways was doing wonders for our relationship. Even though he was impossible sometimes, he was trying. Plus, he realized the one person who had been the biggest threat to me was dead. He would never harm me again.

Megan was shaping up to be a great new addition to the shop, proving she took her job seriously, coming up with new ideas all the time. She asked if I ever considered expanding, maybe adding on to the existing building. Coincidently, there was an empty lot next door, but I didn't have the money in the budget to do anything so grand yet. I refrained from mentioning her idea to Alek because I knew he would buy it before I even had the chance to dispute it. Full Bloom was my baby, and I needed to nurture it my way. I wanted to do it on my own.

We decided to meet at Laverty's, a nice, quaint Irish pub. I'd only been there once, but the finger food certainly left an impression.

The evening was shaping up to be a fun time out, the conversation flowing between us as the hours ticked by.

"So, Megan, did you like living in North Carolina? I've always wanted to visit but never had the opportunity."

She hesitated for a brief moment, looking away as if she didn't know how to answer. Being someone who had skeletons in her own closet, I recognized the fleeting look on her face. Maybe she moved to Seattle because she was trying to escape something, or someone. Much like I had.

Taking a sip of my drink, I allowed her the time she needed to answer me. "I did, although I didn't live there for too long." She avoided my eyes once again, staring instead at the glass of wine in front of her. Deciding best not to push her, I changed the topic.

"Do you have any siblings? Are both of your parents still living?" My questions were innocent enough, but again she looked uneasy. Something about her reactions piqued my curiosity. I'd told Alek I'd done the background check on her, but I didn't. It was on my to-do list. I had, however, called all of her references, and they had nothing but nice things to say about her. I didn't lie about that part, at least.

"Both of my parents are still alive. They're actually still married, if you can believe it." A faint smile spread across her face.

"That's sweet."

Squirming in her chair, she turned the questions on me, "So, what about you, Sara? Does your family live close by?" she asked, bringing her drink to her lips. Her study of me was quite intent, more so than usual.

Maybe I was reading too much into her behavior, Alek's insistence about her background check playing over and over in my head.

Before I could answer, my phone vibrated on top of the table. Taking a quick peek, I saw it was Alek. "Sorry, one sec, Megan." Turning my head to the side, I answered. "Hello. Hey, babe. Yeah, we're having a great time," I said, glancing back at Megan as I spoke. A pissed-off look washed over her face as she realized who I was talking to.

When she saw my questioning look, her scowl quickly switched to a strained smile. I turned my body to the right as I answered him, doing my best not to witness any more of Megan's facial expressions. "Yeah,

I have. One. Don't start," I huffed. "Fine. Okay, I'll call you when we're done. Love you, too." I turned to face her again as I disconnected the call. "Sorry. Alek was just checking in."

"You mean checking up, don't you?" she argued. "Why do you let him get away with that type of behavior?" Draining the rest of my drink, she held my stare and waited for an answer.

"He's not doing anything but looking out for me. I've been through a lot and he's concerned." I didn't particularly care for her tone when she was prying into my business.

"Oh?" she probed. "What happened to you, Sara? Do tell." There was an air of cockiness surrounding her. Or was I reading her wrong? We were having a great time until she started with her interrogation.

"I'm not comfortable talking about it, so let's change the subject. Okay?" Once she realized I wasn't going to divulge something so personal, her demeanor changed a little.

"Sure. Sorry, I don't mean to be so pushy. I think I've had a bit too much to drink." She genuinely smiled that time.

After another half-hour of chatting about clothes and movies, we decided to call it a night. I texted Alek the name of the restaurant, but told Megan if she was ready to go, I would be fine waiting by myself until he got there.

"Actually, Megan, if you want, we can drop you off at home. I don't really think you should be driving."

"Oh, please, this is nothing, girl. I'm completely fine." When I quirked my brow, she said, "Really. I'm fine. I wouldn't drive if I didn't think I could." Knowing she had two glasses of wine was concerning but not overly so. She was a grown woman and I couldn't force her to do anything. Besides, if she was in the same car with Alek, something bad might happen. Her dislike for him continued to baffle me.

"Okay, but only if you're sure."

"I'm positive. I'm actually going to stay for a bit longer anyway. There is a handsome man at the bar who has been checking me out all night." She subtly pointed toward the guy she was referring to. He *was* quite the looker. I didn't blame her. "He looks like Mr. Right Now." She laughed. Gathering her things, she winked at me as she wrangled herself out of our booth.

As we said our goodbyes, Alek called to tell me he was waiting outside. "Okay, well, I had fun, Megan. We'll have to do this again sometime soon."

"You bet we will," she agreed before pulling me in for a quick hug.

Touching her arm, I pleaded, "Please, be careful."

"I will. Don't worry about me. I control my life and everything in it, Sara. Remember that." Before I could dissect her words, she smiled and made her way toward the man who'd caught her attention.

Heading outside, my thoughts were suddenly bombarded with images of my man. I was already excited and I hadn't even laid eyes on him yet.

When he saw me coming, he immediately opened the passenger door for me. Always the gentleman.

"I've missed you, babe," he groaned before gathering me in his arms for a heart-stopping kiss. His hands lowered to grip my ass, pressing me firmly against his body.

"I missed you, too, but if you don't stop it, all these people are going to watch a show." Giving him a quick kiss, I backed up because what I had planned for him should only be done in private.

"Okay, okay. Let's get you home then."

~32~

Alek

It'd been a couple of weeks since Sara and I had officially rekindled our relationship and I couldn't be happier. We were even better than before because we didn't take anything for granted. Mainly because we both knew what it was like to lose the other.

Running from meeting to meeting did nothing to calm the incessant need I had to check on something. Or should I say someone? I tried to ask Sara nicely for Megan's information but she refused to give it to me, trying to play the 'It's insulting you don't trust I'll do my homework' bit. Yeah, I wasn't buying it. I vowed the day she took me back I would never let anyone or anything harm her again.

I couldn't pinpoint what it was about Megan that bothered me. Yes, I found it odd she disliked me so much, especially since I didn't even know her, but it was more than that. There was an uneasiness, trying to tell me there might be trouble ahead.

Call it paranoia.

Call it my innate need to protect my woman.

So, Sara could be upset with me, but I was going to get my hands on that information somehow. And if it wasn't going to be from her, then I was going to approach someone who was as concerned about her safety as I was.

Matt.

I arrived at Full Bloom when I knew Sara was going to be out running some errands. She made sure to keep in touch with me, especially when she wasn't at the shop. Controlling her wasn't my objective. Not at all. I made sure to answer my phone each time she called me, in case she needed me, for whatever might come up.

Walking inside the shop was kind of weird at first, knowing I wasn't there to see Sara. There were only two other customers inside, both of whom were men. I didn't even dwell on the fact my woman was sometimes surrounded by other guys, most of whom came in because they fucked up with their own women. Pushing my crazy thoughts aside, I approached the one person I was curious about.

Megan.

She didn't see me at first because her eyes were glued to one guy's ass as he bent over to select an arrangement from the bottom shelf of the cooler.

To look at her, one would think she was attractive. She was taller than Sara with a little heavier build, blonde curls lying above her collarbone. She was plain, but pretty. Nothing compared to Sara, of course, but I was sure she didn't have an issue garnering a man's attention.

There was a big smile on her face as she continued to watch the man standing to my left. Only when I cleared my throat did she swing her eyes to me, an instant look of disgust contorting her face.

In turn, I chose not to hide my annoyance with her rudeness. "Megan, is it?" I asked, striding toward the counter. Admittedly, I wasn't used to women not fawning all over me. Not that I wanted her to act in such a manner, but it was always easier to obtain information when people were tripping over themselves merely because I paid attention to them.

"Sara's not here," she sneered, focusing her attention back on the computer and completely ignoring me.

She obviously thinks she's done talking to me.

"Have I done something to offend you?" I asked in the most sincere tone I could muster, making a real effort to find out what her problem with me was. My instinct was to be rude and condescending, but I knew it wouldn't work to my advantage.

"Nothing to *me*," she scoffed. She finally lifted her gaze from the screen and glared at me. She literally glared at me. "I don't like you, and you'll reap what you sow."

What the fuck does that mean?

Her unnerving statement solidified she was certainly a little unstable. She may have been able to hide it well from Sara, but she'd shown me her true colors.

Not wanting to entertain her any longer, I walked toward the back of the shop.

"Hey, you can't go back there!" she yelled, rushing to catch up with me. She was close on my heels as I rounded the corner to the prep room. "I said you can't come back here." I whipped around so quickly she had to take a step back.

"I can come and go as I please. Just ask your *boss*." Thankfully, Matt was coming out of the restroom, saving me from telling her to go to hell. He looked quickly between the two of us, clearly confused why we were shouting at each other.

Matt and I hadn't always gotten along. Actually, that was an understatement. We almost came to blows a couple of times, mostly because I overreacted to certain situations. My feelings for Sara were so new and confusing, they twisted me up inside.

Matt still looked confused as he started to speak. "Sara's not here right now, but she'll be back soon. I can tell her you stopped by, though." He glanced down at the sheet in his hand, figuring our conversation was done.

"Actually, I came to see you." I didn't even have to look behind me to know Megan was still shooting daggers at me. "I was going to head over to Verdana later tonight and wanted to know if you could meet me there? I thought we could grab a beer and chat."

Yes, my request was out of left field, and it wasn't lost on Matt.

"Uhhhhh," he stammered. "Yeah...I suppose." His brow furrowed as he asked me, "What time?"

"Meet me there at seven. Do you know where it is?"

"Yes."

No other words were necessary.

The plan was set.

~~~~

I was sitting at the bar drinking a beer when Matt walked up behind me. He was nothing if not punctual. Even though I was going to pump him for information, essentially asking him to go behind Sara's back, I was going to make a real attempt to try and get to know him.

After ordering a draft, Matt took a seat next to me, still trying to figure out why I'd asked him to join me. Sara was shocked as hell when I told her, so I could only imagine what was running through Matt's head.

I wasn't one to beat around the bush, so I got right to it. "Matt, I'm sure you're wondering why I asked you to meet me tonight."

"I *was* wondering...yes," he replied, taking another drink as he waited for my reason.

"Well, as you know, I'll go to extremes to make sure Sara is safe, even when they're things she objects to. We clash heads a lot because of it." I laughed, picturing the many times Sara and I bickered over my antics and her stubbornness.

Matt smirked, because he knew I spoke the truth. He'd been privy to a few of those disagreements.

"What do you need from me?" He sure got right to the point. I liked it. Placing his drink back on the bar, he swiveled around until he was fully facing me. As I attempted to answer his question, his mouth fell open and he rushed to ask, "She's not in any more danger is she?" His voice took on a panicked tremor, and I knew right then how much Sara meant to him. He'd become so worried about his friend, it physically shook him.

"I'm not sure yet." Shaking my head, I tried to clarify. "What I mean is I don't know anything about this new employee of hers. This Megan Smith." I tried to hold back my contempt but it spewed forth, out of my control. "I'd like to do a thorough background check, but of course, Sara refuses to give me her information." Taking another tug off my bottle, I grasped his shoulder. "This is where you come in."

It took him a second to figure out what I was asking him. "Wait, you want me to go behind her back and give you Megan's information?" He blew out a breath and grabbed the back of his neck. "I don't know, man. I don't want her to think she can't trust me. What if she finds out?"

"*If* she finds out, I'll deal with it. I'll make it so you're not to blame at all."

We sat in silence for what seemed like forever. Begging wasn't my style and he knew it. My hope was that he would see the importance of doing the check and agree without any further argument.

"I don't think you're going to find anything more than Sara did. Megan seems harmless to me." He downed the rest of his beer and motioned to the bartender for another. Our conversation was going better than I thought it would. Matt was a pretty good guy after all. "The only issue I had with Megan," he continued, "was convincing her I wasn't interested." He laughed as he took a big swig of his beer.

A couple of minutes passed as we sat in a somewhat-awkward silence. I was giving him time to think on it while I enjoyed the new foreign beer we were trying out. "So...what do you say, Matt? Will you help me?

Thankfully, he didn't make me wait long for an answer. "Yeah, okay. I'll text it to you tomorrow." After exchanging information, I sat back and breathed a sigh of relief.

Leaning over, I bumped his shoulder with mine and asked, "So, Megan was really barking up the wrong tree, wasn't she?" My laughter caused Matt to relax even more.

"Yeah, she was." Then all of a sudden, his brow furrowed in confusion. "Wait. What?"

"You're not interested in Megan, correct?" *Shit!* I didn't mean to call him out. Obviously, he wasn't ready to make it known he wasn't attracted to women.

"No, I'm not," he answered flatly.

"Well then, she's barking up the wrong tree, right?" I asked him again, hopefully that time a little less obvious.

"Yeah, you're right." He gulped down the last of his drink and stood up. "Well, I have to be going. I'll send you her info tomorrow."

"Great. Thanks, Matt," I said, shaking his hand.

My fears were soon going to be laid to rest.

~33~

Sara

A week had gone by. Work was busy, as usual, thank God. Alek and I had been spending all of our free time together. Life was good. But it became even better...when Alek proposed.

That we live together.

For good.

It was a no-brainer.

I said yes right away.

I'd been staying at his house almost every night, so the move made sense.

We were it for each other.

At first, I was hesitant to broach the subject with Alexa, even though I was sure she knew it was coming. I still felt bad leaving her all alone in the apartment. As soon as I found enough courage to talk to her about it, she shut me down, telling me it was about time.

Figuring it was as good a time as any, she informed me she and Braden were having the same exact conversation, with one minor difference. She wasn't quite sure if she wanted to take the leap yet. Braden was pushing for it, but my dear friend was afraid of losing herself in the relationship. She wanted to still keep her independence, something Braden was trying to be understanding about.

I was lost in thought when a voice startled me.

"Sara? Did you hear me? Did you want to go?"

I turned around to see Megan hovering over my right shoulder, watching me put together an order for a delivery.

"Huh?" I asked, continuing to arrange the gardenias until they were perfect. "Sorry, Megan. What did you ask me?"

She sighed, almost as if she was annoyed. But her tone when she spoke again was anything but. "I asked if you wanted to go to Throttle tonight. There's a new band playing I'm dying to check out." Rocking back and forth on her heels, she asked, "So, what do you say? Are you in?"

My first thought was that Alek might end up showing up at the club, being the owner and everything, and what kind of tension it would cause between the two of them. But the bigger Megan's smile became, the less I worried about it.

"Sure. Sounds like fun. Why don't we invite Alexa and Matt to go with us? They love Throttle, and I'm sure they would be up for some new musical talent."

Again, she looked annoyed, but as soon as she smiled, I thought I'd misread her.

"Great. You can let them know we'll be meeting up at eight-thirty. The band doesn't go on until ten, but I thought we could relax and hang out before they start." Our conversation ended when she took off to help the customer who had walked in.

~~~~

The night had been going well. Everyone was laughing and telling stories, mainly about some asinine customers who had come into the shop. Thankfully, there weren't too many of them to regale.

"Then, as he was asking me to fill out the card for him—for his wife, mind you—he asked if I was free later that night." Megan grimaced as she told us her story.

"What an ass," Alexa bemused. "Guys are creeps."

"Hey," Matt fussed. "Not all of us are creeps. Some of us are good guys, you know." Even though Matt was smiling, he looked as if something was bothering him. Matter of fact, he'd been wearing the same look on his face for a while now. Trying to convince him to open up and talk about it was like pulling teeth. Worse even. He'd shut down if I pressed too much. I assumed he would talk when he was ready.

"Some of you are all right," Megan chirped, smiling wide in Matt's direction. I'd seen her curiosity at the way the three of us interacted together.

Matt was like our brother, warning off unwanted attention. There were obviously no romantic intentions flitting around our group. Well...with the exception of Megan, I supposed. The way she watched my friend was a little sad, only because she seemed to really like him. The one thing he did open up to me about was when he had to shoot down her advances toward him, an awkward situation for sure because he didn't want to hurt her feelings. But she was always touching him and asking if he wanted to grab drinks after work. He let her down easy, though, stating he only viewed her as a friend and nothing more.

But tell that to her heart. Or was it another body part which needed to be told?

She watched him when he flung his arm around Alexa's shoulder, pulling her in close to give her a kiss on the cheek. He'd done the same thing with me earlier.

As the night wore on, the more Megan's mood seemed to sour. I didn't know if it was because Matt wasn't paying her as much attention as he was to Alexa and me, or if there was something else bothering her altogether.

"Can we move closer?" Alexa asked as she grabbed my hand, already pulling me forward before I even answered. "I hear these guys are amazing!" she shouted over her shoulder.

Megan and Matt followed us as we approached the stage. The band was busy chatting with some patrons while they set up their equipment.

An hour into the show, I suddenly became a little woozy. I tried to blame it on the alcohol, especially since I hadn't eaten in hours. Drinking on an empty stomach was never a good idea. Taking some deep breaths, praying it would do the trick, I fumbled to find something to lean against. There were so many people crowding me, it was hard to breathe. Add in my sudden attack of dizziness and it didn't make for a good time.

Staggering toward the edge of the bar, I accidentally bumped into Megan, spilling a bit of her drink on the floor. My other friends were turned away from me, thoroughly enjoying the music to even notice I wasn't okay. She looked annoyed at first then concern washed over her as she saw me swaying where I stood. And it certainly wasn't because of the music.

I knew something was wrong. My mind instantly flew to thinking someone had spiked my drink. But I reasoned it was impossible since the only people who had touched it before me were the bartender, Matt and Megan. They had each bought a round for the group. In fact, it was Alexa's turn to buy next.

"Sara, are you okay?" Megan asked, shoving her shoulder under my arm to try and keep me steady. Her support of my body was a relief, and I leaned into her even more. I was terrified I was going to face-plant right there, in front of everyone.

My head spun.

My muscles were like jelly.

My body started to heat up and my vision became cloudy.

My eyes glanced over at Megan, and in a split-second I saw a strange expression cross her face. I didn't have the energy to read into it because it was gone not a moment later.

Suddenly, pain radiated across my cheek. Confusion swept over me as I stared at the woman holding me up. She'd slapped me in an attempt to keep me coherent.

"Sara, you don't look well. Do you want to go home?" I heard Alexa's voice behind me, but she sounded so far away. It was almost as if I was dreaming. I couldn't focus on anything, all of the people around me blurring into one large mass.

In a way, I was frozen.

I was unable to turn around.

I couldn't speak to tell my best friend something was wrong.

The last thing I heard was Megan telling her she would take me outside, that she lived around the corner and would pump me full of coffee, sobering me up and returning me to our night out.

Promising we would be back in an hour, Megan ushered me from the club.

It was the last thing I remembered before darkness dragged me under.

~34~

Alek

It was past midnight and I hadn't heard from Sara yet. Nothing. Not a text or a phone call to let me know she was all right. Didn't she know what a mess I would be, leaving me totally in the dark as to what was going on with her? I wasn't asking her to call me every hour or anything so extreme, but a simple check-in every five hours wasn't asking too much. I didn't think so, anyway.

As I picked up my phone to try her, it rang. *Thank God.* I glanced down at the name displayed across the screen and my heart picked up speed.

It wasn't Sara at all.

It was Calvin.

I was still waiting on information about Megan. The strange feeling I'd been harboring simply wouldn't go away. Instinctually, I knew there was more to her story than she revealed to Sara. I was hoping it was something small, but my gut was telling me I should be wary.

And I always followed my gut when it came to the woman I love.

"Devera," I practically shouted into the phone. I was already pacing back and forth and he hadn't even uttered a single word.

"Alek," he said pensively. "Is Sara with you right now?" The tremor in his voice made my heart constrict. There was obviously something wrong if the first words out of his mouth pertained to Sara's whereabouts.

"No, she's not. Why? Tell me what you know." I was becoming increasingly agitated, my fear overwhelming me to the point I could barely catch my breath.

"I did a thorough background check on Megan Smith and at first, there wasn't anything alarming. She had no priors. Nothing unusual. Until I dug further back and realized she changed her name eight years ago." The silence was deafening. I had no idea where he was going with his story, but mentioning *eight years ago* instantly raised the hair on the back of my neck. "Alek, her name used to be Denise Colden."

The world spun around me.

There was no way. It had to be a coincidence. *Don't freak out.* As much as I tried to convince myself there had to be another explanation, I knew better.

"Is it her?" I asked, my voice dripping with worry. "Is Megan Samuel's sister?"

I knew the answer, but hearing him say it was still a shock.

"Yes."

All those years before, I'd done my research. I knew everything about Samuel Colden, mainly in part due to Calvin's expertise. I knew everything about his family, including his sister Denise. *Or should I say Megan?* I knew his family received death threats for what he'd done to Sara. I was assuming it was why she changed her name, but who the hell knew.

I should have been more persistent in finding out about her. Or at the very least, I should have asked Matt for Megan's information immediately after Sara's refusal.

"I don't understand, Cal. What could she want with Sara?"

"Not sure. Maybe she blames Sara for her brother's death? All I know is that she changed her name right after he was put away for kidnapping her, probably because her family was receiving death threats." *Bingo.* "Their parents passed away a few years back, so Samuel was the only family she had left. And now..."

We both knew what came after *and now.*

And now, she blames Sara for her brother's death.

And now, she is going to exact revenge.

But *I* was the one responsible for killing Samuel. Me. Not Sara. So why not come after me?

A sickening thought rattled my brain as I tried to take in everything. She *was* coming after me. By tricking Sara into thinking they were friends, she was going to use her as bait. To get to me.

The realization both infuriated and relieved me. If Megan's attention was truly aimed at me, then Sara would still be alive.

If my hunch was correct.

Quickly ending the call with Calvin, I grabbed my keys and rushed out of the house.

I had to find her, before it was too late.

Trying to call her proved futile.

There was no answer, as I knew there wouldn't be.

Racing toward Throttle, I prayed no harm had come to her. I didn't think I would survive another devastation.

I barely held it together last time when she'd been shot.

~35~

Sara

What was with me waking up with mind-splitting headaches? I made sure not to overdo it, but there I was again. Temples throbbing and a dizziness which instantly made me sick to my stomach.

It took me awhile to realize I wasn't lying down. Instead, I was sitting upright on something cold and hard, my limbs immobile. My eyes were still closed and I couldn't really hear anything. It was quiet.

Eerily quiet.

Where the hell am I? How did I get here? The last memory I had was getting ready to go out, to meet everyone at Throttle. That was where the recollections became fuzzy.

Finally, I heard a faint noise, running water off in the distance. It was muffled but I could make it out. Definitely water.

Then I hear a door open and close, someone slowly walking toward me and then... nothing. Back to silence. I thought I imagined everything until I heard a voice.

"Welcome back to the land of the living. For now, at least." Megan was the person behind the voice, but why was she speaking in such a hateful tone?

"Megan? Where are we? Why can't I remember anything? Are you all right?" I asked, my speech slurring with each syllable. I knew something was seriously wrong, but I held tight to the hope everything would be explained and there was a good reason for it all.

"I'm fine, Sara," she said, my name disdainful on her lips. "You're the one who's not."

She moved around me with stealth-like precision. I barely heard her footsteps before my head was violently forced back, my chair almost tipped over with the force. I cried out, but it only fueled her anger more. She loved the fact she was hurting me, but for the life of me I couldn't understand why.

When she let go, I sprang forward and quickly righted myself. I was so weak, but I forced my body to cooperate. Forcing my eyes open proved painful, but I needed to see her.

I needed to see what she was going to do to me.

As soon as my lids popped open, they closed just as fast. The bright light was killing me, causing my headache to spike again. When I tried to shield my eyes with my hands, I realized I couldn't move them. They were restrained behind my back.

"I don't understand, Megan. Please...please, tell me what's going on."

To say I was confused was an understatement.

"You want to know what's going on?" she asked, hitting me in the back of the head with her hand. Circling around to stand in front of me, she squatted and looked me in the face, her eyes so glazed over, I was positive she had taken something. "Well, let me tell you a story. Once upon a time, there was a little girl who had a big brother, a brother who did his best to protect her. But there was something off about him, something everyone knew about, yet they still made fun of him. But he couldn't help the way he was. It wasn't his fault." Her voice cracked, indicating this story was indeed a personal one.

"Then one day, he did something beyond his control because he thought he was in love. He took a girl to his house and because she was there for a short time, everyone panicked and caused the situation to escalate. They called him names and hurt him, locking him away for eight years, probing him and forcing countless drugs down his throat. They even closed him off from the only remaining family he had left. Me."

As I tried to listen to her story, the only person who popped into my head was Samuel. But it was impossible. He only had one sister and her name was Denise. The only reason I knew was because I was afraid his family was going to retaliate on me somehow, so I asked the police for as much information as they could give me. Thankfully, nothing ever happened.

Until now.

My eyes had finally adjusted to the bright light in the room, allowing me to see Megan standing in front of me, a knife held tightly in her hand.

I finally realized how dire my situation was right then.

"Megan, I don't understand what this has to do with me," I squeaked, afraid if I spoke any louder I'd set her off.

She leaned down and pointed the knife directly in my face, so close if I breathed the wrong way, it would poke me. "I'll tell you how you're involved." She took a deep breath before ranting on. "You were the one who led my brother on. You were the one who gave him false hope. And at the first sign things weren't going your way, you decided to tell the authorities he kidnapped you. You stole him away from me!" she hollered. "*You* did that."

"Megan, please. I liked Samuel. I did. But he was sick. He thought we were in a relationship, and he forced me to stay with him against my will." I didn't even finish before she flipped out.

"STOP!" she roared. Before I could take my next breath, a burning sensation ripped through my arm. Warm liquid seeped out and dripped to the floor. She'd lost control for a split-second and cut me. "Stop telling me lies. We both know what happened."

My eyes cautiously studied her movements as she paced in front of me. She wielded the knife as if it would deliver the truth. Her version of the truth. Glancing down at my arm made me wince. It hurt like hell because it was more than a superficial wound. Multiple stitches would be required to seal the flesh back together.

Another scar from the past I can't seem to escape from.

"The day they released my brother was the best day ever," she remembered, a small, crazy smile on her face as she thought of Samuel. She looked away, lost in a memory which caused her to tear up. "I loved him, Sara. He was my big brother." She looked like the old Megan for a second.

"I'm so sorry," I said, my words having the opposite effect.

"Sorry?" she screamed. "Sorry? Did you honestly just say that to me, you deceitful bitch?" She swung her fist at me, hitting me right in the temple and knocking me to the floor. "You and your bastard boyfriend are responsible for my brother's death," she sneered, a look of pure rage contorting her face. "And now both of you will pay."

Lying on my side, I tried everything I could to remain as calm as possible, doing my best not to pass out. I needed to remain alert, especially since she mentioned exacting revenge on Alek as well as me.

All of a sudden, my cell phone started ringing. Wasting no time, Megan stalked toward my purse and grabbed my phone.

"Well, lookey here. It's the man of the hour," she taunted, preparing to answer it.

"Megan, what are you doing? Leave him out of it. You have me. If you want to take out your anger on anyone, take it out on me. Please,"

I cried, but my pleas fell on deaf ears. She shot me an annoyed look, answering my phone in the sweetest of voices.

"Alek, thank God you called. Yes, Sara is with me. She wasn't feeling the best, so I brought her back to my apartment to sober up before we went back." She was silent as she listened to whatever he was saying. *What the hell is he saying?*

Her next words broke me. "Why don't you come and pick her up then? Yes." She glanced at me as her lips turned up in an evil smirk. "I'll be waiting for you." She gave him the address before ending the call. We were ten minutes from Throttle, which meant it would take him thirty minutes to arrive. She could do all sorts of things to me in that time.

"Megan, please, don't do this. Please," I begged her. I couldn't bear to drag Alek into yet another dangerous situation, but my hands were tied. Literally. I was still lying on my side when Megan advanced in my direction. Seeing as how this wouldn't be the best presentation for when Alek arrived, she bent down and lifted me back upright.

As soon as she turned her back to me, I fiddled with the rope which bound my hands to the chair. Soon, I was able to loosen the knot she made. Not enough to escape. Not yet, at least.

"I knew Alek would come for you without question. He'll always come for his precious Sara," she scoffed, hate laced around each word.

"Please, don't involve him. It wasn't his fault. It was mine."

"He shot and killed my brother. How is it not his fault?" She breached the distance between us with a few angry steps. The knife was pointed right in my face. "How? Tell me right now before I slice that pretty face of yours."

I trembled and hated myself for showing weakness. For some odd reason, I knew my weakness would only fuel her vendetta even more. "I was the one who misled Samuel," I confessed, knowing I was only lying to try and buy more time. "I was the one responsible for his death, Megan. It was all my fault and I'm sorry."

My lies permeated her crazy brain. I knew enough from watching plenty of shows on people who have snapped to not stick with your version of the story. If they believed it to be one way, you had to find a common link to keep you alive. But how long would it work? I had no idea, but I had to give it a shot.

"He loved you, Sara. All he wanted was to be with you. You should have stayed with him this time."

The bitch was stone-cold out of her mind. But at least I was buying myself some time.

She continued to shake her head in confusion as she made her way down the long hallway. She entered what I could only assume was her bathroom and slammed the door behind her. I went to work on the rope with enhanced fervor, trying to give myself the best fighting chance, only stopping when I heard a noise behind me.

"Sara." I heard someone whisper my name, but I thought I was hallucinating. Whatever Megan gave me was strong enough to knock me out, then keep my head fuzzy when I came to. I continued to work on my restraints. "Sara." I heard it again. I turned my head to the side and couldn't believe who I saw.

Brian was crouched in the window, prying the rest of it open as quietly as possible so as not to alert Megan. He must have been watching long enough to know when to make his move. For a brief moment, I was brought back to the night Samuel had managed to hit him in the head, before abducting me. I cringed at the thought he was putting himself in danger yet again...for me.

"Brian," I cried out, clasping my lips together as soon as I made the noise. I turned my head toward the hallway to make sure she hadn't heard me. So far, so good. He raised the window the rest of the way so he could fit through.

He was on me in two seconds flat, working the rope from its knot in even quicker time. Once my wrists were free, I grabbed them and rubbed feverishly, forcing the blood to flow freely. "How did you find me so fast? Alek just called here." As soon as I tried to stand, I fell right back down. I wasn't strong enough to move on my own.

"Alek called me as soon as he found out Megan was Samuel's sister." I looked on in confusion. "He told me what I needed to know. He gave me your coordinates and I rushed right over. I was instructed to do everything humanly possible to get you out of here alive." Helping me to stand again, he assured me Alek was going to be there any minute.

It was an assurance which made me fearful.

As Brian tried to usher me toward the front door, Megan came tearing down the hall, wielding that damn knife and threatening to do some damage.

"What the fuck are you doing? Move away from her before I kill you both." She advanced on us, anger and craziness mixed together to form the most deadly concoction.

The front door crashed open before she reached us. The loud noise startled all three of us, and for a split-second, time stood still.

Alek crouched in the doorway, assessing the situation for what it was. Dangerous. He saw the knife in Megan's hand then rested his eyes on my arm. There was still a steady flow of blood dripping from my wound.

Without hesitation, he pushed off the door frame and ran straight at Megan.

"Alek, no!" I screamed, but it was too late. He had rushed her and knocked her to the ground, her head bouncing off the hard floor before she was knocked out cold.

When I glanced back at Alek, I saw there was a confused look on his face but I couldn't figure out why. Until I ran my eyes down the full length of his body only to come across a horrific sight.

The knife Megan had brandished was plunged into his stomach. Only the handle was visible. Screams tore from me as he fell to his knees. I tried to rush to him, but my body wasn't cooperating. Falling to the ground, I did my best to crawl toward the man I loved.

Toward the man who had given his life for me.

~36~

Alek

Images of Sara in distress kept flashing through my head. For a brief moment, I saw her slumped in her chair, barely having enough strength to sit upright. Blood oozed from a pretty nasty cut on her arm, dark liquid torturing me as it fell from her body. Her eyes were hazy at best as she tried to take in the scene around her.

Then I saw Megan. And the knife. Allowing my rage to take over like a beast I'd tried to keep at bay for far too long, I lunged forward with no regard for my own safety. My only goal was to ensure Sara made it out of there alive.

Thankfully, Brian had been able to at least untie her, even though she could barely keep from falling over. Whatever that bitch gave her was enough to slow down any natural reaction she would have normally had. Her body wasn't her own, and I was sure she was terrified.

I never made eye contact with her as I rushed to put an end to Megan's crazy rant. Knowing the pain and worry in her eyes would make me falter, I focused on one thing and one thing only.

Removing the threat from my woman.

So many thoughts ran through me, almost like a bombardment of memories since the first day I'd officially met Sara. They were all jumbled together, though, and I couldn't make sense of any of it.

A searing pain shot through my stomach and I tried to clutch the area with my hands, but I found I couldn't reach it. In fact, there wasn't a single part of my body following my brain's instruction to move.

A faint noise sounded somewhere in the background, the odd pitch of the beeping confusing me as to where I was.

Is my alarm going off?

Then I heard the sweetest voice.

My Sara.

"Doctor, when do you think he'll wake up?" I heard her say, the fear in her voice instantly making me nervous.

But why?

I was only sleeping.

Wait, why was there a doctor in my bedroom?

Where the hell am I? All of a sudden, everything came crashing back full-force, images hitting me so fast I couldn't differentiate what was real and what wasn't. I remembered busting down a door, my eyes flying to Brian and Sara, before rushing forward. The next memory which strangled me was being on my back and glancing at something sticking out of my stomach. A silver handle, but I had no idea what it was. I didn't remember feeling anything. No pain.

My body reacted to the intrusion all the same. Tunnel vision racked my sight and before I could open my mouth to say anything, the cruel grips of darkness dragged me under.

Wherever I was, I was okay. At least I could still hear her angelic voice, the lilt of her tone soothing my frantic nerves. Realizing Sara was not only alive, but unharmed enough to speak on my behalf, gave me comfort.

"It's hard to say. He had a close call, Miss Hawthorne. The surgery went as planned, but now it's up to him. Sometimes, a trauma such as his causes the body to go into shock to protect itself." There was a brief silence and I swore I heard Sara crying. "We'll have to wait and see what happens. The good news is he's stable and we're keeping a close eye on him."

He must have walked out of the room because the only sound I heard was the incessant beeping near my head. *I'm obviously lying in a hospital bed.* I wanted so badly to wake up and hold her in my arms, professing everything would be all right. I wanted to tell her how much I loved her and I would gladly risk my life over and over if it meant protecting her.

But no matter how hard I tried, I couldn't move one single muscle. It was a funny thing to have your own body betray you. Frustration mounted, but there wasn't a damn thing I could do about it.

I was tired, even though I wasn't technically awake. Using what little mental energy I had sapped all of my strength. Instead of focusing on the fact I couldn't wake up, I chose to concentrate on Sara's breathing. Her fingertips drew nervous circles over the top of my hand. All I wanted to do was grab her and pull her close. But I couldn't.

Over the next couple of hours, or it could have been minutes for all I knew, quite a few people came into my room. Some of them I recognized but some I did not.

Sleep took hold when I couldn't will myself to stay alert any longer. Alert. I was far from it, but inside my own head, I was aware of everything going on around me. Sara's sadness washed over her. I swear my heart picked up pace, but there was no outward indication of such. No monitors going off around me to let her know I heard her voice or felt her sweet touch.

I can hear you, baby.

Since I was powerless inside my own body, I gave in to the calm and drifted off into dreams of holding Sara close.

~37~

Sara

I was going out of my mind. I prayed every day Alek would wake up, and each day I was let down. I'd cried so much over the past week, helpless as I saw him lying there, I didn't think I had a single tear left.

I was done. For the rest of my life, I would never be able to cry ever again.

So many emotions whirled through me, threatening to take me down if I didn't get a grip. I was fearful I would never be able to tell him I loved him again. Shutting down inside, I couldn't face the fact I might never feel his touch again. The only realization to come out of the situation was I knew exactly how he felt when I'd jumped in front of him when Samuel had pulled the trigger. He was so angry with me for putting my life in danger, an emotion I returned ten-fold. I wanted him to wake up so I could tell him how upset I was with him. I wished for him to argue right back with me. Giving anything to hear his voice again, it would make me the happiest woman alive.

Hope he would wake slowly diminished with each passing day, but I kept on trudging through. I would never give up on him. Not as long as his heart beat in tune with mine, or breath still filled his lungs.

The doctor told me they had to remove his spleen because the knife had caused too much damage. There had also been some damage to his large intestine, but they were able to repair the tear rather easily. Then, when I thought he was out of the woods, an infection took hold, but thankfully they were able to control it.

I was constantly reassured his stats were stable. He just wouldn't wake the hell up. Only he could decide when it was time to come back to me.

It was all a waiting game.

Matt had been a dream. Not only had he spent countless hours at the hospital with me, but he was running the shop all by himself in my absence. We had some part-time helpers who also stepped up, working more hours to make sure the business wasn't negatively affected. When I told him I would have no problem closing the doors of Full Bloom until Alek was better, he told me I was crazy. He said he welcomed the distraction, a far-off look sweeping over him before he pulled me into one of the many hugs we'd shared over the weeks.

Everyone had stopped by the hospital countless times to check on his progress, but the diagnosis remained the same. No change. Alexa was there by my side more often than not, sometimes bringing Braden along with her for her own support. It was all too familiar, because it wasn't all that long ago I was the one lying in the hospital bed.

When I laid eyes on Katherine as she walked through the door, I about lost it. Not like it was a hard thing to do, given the situation. Her kind eyes and warm smile made me think of my gram. My heart ached as she pulled me into her embrace, stroking my hair and telling me everything was going to be okay.

Kael and Adara visited their friend often. On many occasions, I had to excuse myself because Kael's grief was too much for me to handle.

Brad and Natalie Collins, his parents' friends who I'd met at the charity gala, stopped by as well, making me promise to call them as soon as anything changed.

When everyone had gone, and it was only Alek and me in his hospital room, I gave in to my grief. Holding his hand in mine, I laid my head down on the edge of his bed and prayed God would answer my prayers and bring him back to me.

~38~

Sara

"Alek, can you hear me? Please, baby. Move your finger if you can hear me." I said the same thing day in and day out, but the results always remained the same. Nothing ever happened. I wasn't even sure if he heard my words.

Hardly ever leaving his bedside, I'd become a permanent fixture there at the hospital. But the staff didn't mind. In fact, it was the wonderful nurses who gave me the extra strength I needed, their words of encouragement boosting my saddened spirit.

As my head rested on the edge of his bed, I heard someone walk into the room behind me.

"Sara? Are you awake?" Alexa whispered as she stepped closer.

Picking my head up, I gingerly glanced to my left and saw my best friend standing there, a change of clothes for me in her hands. I was a mess and she knew it, eating and showering only when people vehemently urged me to do so.

My eyes were red and puffy, my hair its usual tangled mess. Sure I was quite the sight; I couldn't garner enough strength to care.

"Unfortunately, yes, I'm awake." Without warning, I burst into tears. I was exhausted, both physically and mentally. All I wanted to do was join Alek in his coma, only awakening when he'd finally come back to me. My heart broke a little bit more each day he stayed wrapped up in whatever world held him captive.

Alexa immediately approached, seized my shoulders and gave me a big hug. "Come on, Sara" she pleaded, trying her hardest to convince me to stand. "You need a break."

"No," I said, fighting against her. But it wasn't much of a struggle. I barely had enough strength as it was.

"Yes," she demanded more sternly. "I brought you a change of clothes, and some toiletries. You need to take a shower and get yourself together." She plopped a bag full of stuff onto the chair behind her. "Is this the first sight you want Alek to see when he opens his eyes?" she asked, waving her hands up and down my body.

"I'll take one later, Lex."

"No the hell you won't. You'll take one now. All you do is sit by his bed, Sara. You don't leave except when you're made to. You don't eat or drink anything unless you're forced." She placed her hand on my arm in comfort. "You're not taking care of yourself, and it needs to stop."

Before I could protest, she grabbed my arm and forced me to my feet. Snatching the bag she'd brought with her, she dragged me into the small bathroom, placed my necessities on the sink and pulled the door closed behind her as she left me by myself. I heard her say something from the other side but I couldn't quite make it out. Maybe something about keeping watch until I was done?

I was hesitant to leave his bedside, but I knew if Alexa had gone through so much trouble, I surely looked a fright. Glancing into the mirror, I had my answer.

Holy hell! I look like shit!

I allowed the water to work its magic, washing away layer upon layer of hurt and worry, pain and distress. After ten long minutes, I finished up and wrapped a towel around my thinner frame.

As I brushed my hair in the mirror, I thought about how Alek was going to scold me for not taking care of myself. But those thoughts gave me instant comfort. I would welcome every last worried word which fell from his lips if it meant he would wake up and come back to me.

When I was finished, I headed back to his bedside.

Nothing had changed. Alek was still the same. Still lost to me and everyone else who loved him. Alexa was sitting in the chair I had vacated minutes earlier, holding his hand and pleading with him to wake up, that her best friend was broken and she didn't know what to do. It was then I realized I wasn't the only person who was affected by what had happened. I had a family of friends who cared about me as much as they cared about him. They all saw how much I was hurting, and it was devastating to them they couldn't do anything to help ease my pain.

~39~

Alek

Dreams had quickly become my solace. In them, I would simply let go and allow my unconscious self to run wild. I dreamt of when I was a boy goofing off in school with my friends. But when the teacher turned around to scold us, it was Sara. Then all of a sudden, the dream switched to my childhood home. Again, Sara was there with me, holding my hand as we ran through the house. I thought something was chasing us because I'd become panicky, clutching her fingers in mine as I pulled her behind me from room to room.

She was in all of my dreams, some of them in the past while others were in what seemed to be the future. I saw her pregnant with my child, which was odd because I knew how adamantly she didn't want to have kids. I saw her dancing around our kitchen to some crazy song she liked. As I was about to engulf her in my arms, she would slip further and further away from me, calling out to me while she continued to laugh and sing her song.

But there was something wrong with her. She appeared to be in good spirits, but her eyes told a different story. They were lifeless. All of a sudden, my dream turned on me and I was the one sitting by her bedside, holding her hand as I prayed for her to return to me.

Was it a memory or a premonition?

I heard her voice again, but I was no longer dreaming. I was awake. Well...my version of awake, at least. Her smooth voice drifted over me as she cupped my hand. Her touch was so cold I instantly became worried, but with the state I was in, there wasn't a damn thing I could do about it.

I overheard Alexa practically yelling at her to take a shower. I knew she hadn't been taking care of herself, and I was going to make sure to give her an earful the first chance I got.

Hearing her friend plead with me to wake up was heartbreaking. She whispered how afraid and worried she was about Sara, and assured me I was the only one who could fix her. I wanted to scream that I was trying my hardest to come back to her, but my treacherous body wasn't listening to me.

"Everyone keeps telling me I need a break, that I need to go home and sleep, but I can't," Sara whispered, running her thumb over the top of my hand. "What if you wake up when I'm gone, then slip away from me again?" She broke my heart with every word.

I tried to will my mouth to move, to allow words to pass over my lips and give her comfort, but nothing happened. I attempted to force my body to move, but it betrayed me yet again. My efforts soon exhausted me and I had to rest. I needed my strength to try again soon.

~~~~

It was warm. I wanted nothing more than to throw the blanket off me, but I couldn't. I was restricted to endure whatever fate the doctors and nurses deemed necessary. Being increasingly frustrated and angry was becoming quite the norm for me now. If I didn't wake up soon, I was going to be one pissed-off man to contend with.

Deep down, I understood my predicament was my body's way of protecting itself, but fucking enough already. According to my sweet angel, it had been a week since I'd been stabbed.

A week without touching her soft skin.

A week without tasting those delectable lips.

A week of not having her body wrapped around mine while we moved in sync toward ecstasy.

Sara was in the middle of telling me how much she missed me, including my overbearing ways, when I tried yet again to communicate with her somehow. I would take a stupid wiggling of one of my fingers if it meant she would gain the comfort she so desperately needed.

Then it happened.

A simple movement was all it took to break me out of my slumbering world.

My left pointer finger rose off the bed an inch, but it was enough to push her fears away, bringing all hope of recovery forward. I did it again, and again, until she noticed. She was in the middle of a sentence when suddenly she became quiet.

I'm coming back to you, baby.

"Alek? Can you hear me?" she asked, hope laced around each word. "Do it again. Raise your finger for me one more time."

And I did. One more time.

She squealed so loudly that within seconds, there was a nurse rushing into the room. She inquired as to what was wrong, and when Sara explained, the nurse laughed, patted my arm and told her I must've been done with my nap.

She checked my vitals and reported everything looked good. The next step was to wait. *More waiting.* But it was progress, and I latched onto it with all I could.

All of the excitement quickly wore me out, pushing me back into my dreams once again.

~40~

Sara

It was the smallest of movements, but it made my heart soar. Even though a full day had passed, my hope had been restored Alek was on his way back to me.

I was sitting by his bedside, as usual, when he squeezed my hand right when I asked him to. His grip was weak at first, but it didn't matter. He heard me and his body reacted.

His eyes were still closed, never giving way to the struggle he might be going through. I hoped he'd heard each word I'd whispered to him. But I wouldn't know for sure until he woke up, giving me my opportunity to ask him.

I was walking back into the room from a quick bathroom break when I saw his eyelids flutter. Rushing to his side, I stroked his jaw as I encouraged the progress. One after the other, he slowly opened his eyes, looking straight ahead, unable to focus at first.

"That's it, honey. Take your time. I'm right here when you're ready," I cried, pure joy pouring from the depths of my soul.

His lips parted but no sound came out. It took him awhile before he was finally able to shift his head to the side. The moment his eyes found mine was glorious. I witnessed my undying love reflected back at me.

How I'd missed those beautiful, soul-searching green eyes of his. I was beginning to think I would never see them again. But there he was, looking right at me, pleading with me to be more patient with him as his body began the process of waking up.

Refusing to overwhelm him with my incessant need to rain kisses all over his face, I leaned over and pushed the button for the nurse. I caressed his cheek again, a weeks' worth of beard growth scratchy against my skin. The nurses made sure to keep him looking as much like himself while he recuperated, so they shaved him weekly, asking me multiple times if I wanted to do it instead. But I didn't trust myself. I knew from my lack of sleep and nutrition, I wouldn't be able to keep my hand steady enough to pull off the job. So I relied on them for their kindness.

Alek had lost weight and looked like a paler, thinner version of himself. To me, he was still the most beautiful man alive. I knew once he was truly on the road to recovery, he was going to push himself until he was back to normal. And I knew it was my job to make sure he didn't overdo it.

"Well, well. Look who's awake." The nurse startled me even though I was the one who called for her. She glanced over at me and smiled, the struggles of the eight days etched deep into the lines on my face.

"Obviously this means he's out of the woods, right?" I asked, hopeful she was going to soothe my tightly wound nerves.

"Well, I don't want to rush things, but yes, this is a good sign." She checked his vitals before typing in the results to the computer she wheeled in behind her. "I'll see if I can find the doctor so he can do his own exam. I'll be back as soon as I can."

After she left, I placed my hand back in his and simply stared at him. I was in awe. All I wanted him to do was speak to me, assure me he was going to be okay. As I parted my lips to speak, his eyes fluttered closed, the excitement obviously too draining on him.

"It's okay, sweetheart. Rest now. You're going to need it." I leaned in and kissed his lips. When I moved back, I saw a small smile tip the corners of his mouth as he drifted off to sleep.

In the next couple of hours, I called everyone I could think of to tell them the good news. They all wanted to rush right over, but it was nearing eight in the evening and visiting hours were almost finished. Plus, he had fallen back asleep, and I didn't want to push too fast.

The next day, Kael came strolling into the room as Alek was waking up.

"Well, my man, if you wanted this kind of attention, there are better ways of going about it." He strode toward me and kissed my cheek, and for some reason, I glanced over at Alek. Sure enough, there was a look of annoyance on his face. But he still wasn't speaking, so he couldn't voice his displeasure. I smiled. He was coming back to me more each day. All of him. His possessiveness over me was the most reassuring, proving we would be back to normal very soon. It would annoy me later on but right then, it made me happy.

Kael caught his look, as well, and patted his arm. "Don't go getting all crazy on me. Actually, nix that. Go ahead, be crazy. At least that way, you'll yell at me, and I would like nothing more than to hear your voice." He moved in closer. "I've missed ya, buddy." Kael had really been affected by Alek's condition. I hadn't realized how close they were until he was hurt. Pain and fear shone in his eyes as he stared at his longtime friend, lying helpless in a hospital bed.

I wanted to comfort him but I had no words, slowly recovering myself each day.

~41~

Sara

Another week had passed since Alek had officially woken up, and I was on cloud nine. He was talking more each day, the sound of his voice like music to my ears.

Friends visited but they were careful not to stay for too long, realizing his recovery was in the beginning stages. I was acutely aware whenever Alek's eyes were following me, even in a room full of people.

Sitting by his bedside for the past couple of weeks, I realized his need to protect me would never go away. It was ingrained in him, even stronger than his own need for survival. Once, he'd woken in a panic, his eyes darting all over the room trying to search for me. His heart rate accelerated and his hand clenched mine in fear. I was able to quickly calm him down, a look of peace restored on his face before he fell back asleep.

I wondered who plagued his nightmares. Was it Samuel or his deranged sister?

Megan was no longer a threat. Kael had informed me after she'd been hauled away, she killed herself a week later while waiting to meet with her lawyer. Somehow, she'd gotten ahold of a small razor blade and ended her life before she rotted away in some prison cell.

No more looking over my shoulder, wondering if the whole tragedy with Samuel was going to continue in some way. Megan was the last of his family who would exact revenge for him.

It was done.

Finally.

"What are you so happy about today?" Alek asked, bringing me back from my thoughts. I hadn't even known he'd woken up.

"Isn't it obvious?" I leaned forward and gently kissed him hello. His tongue parted his mouth and ran along my bottom lip. It appeared he was feeling better.

"Are you happy because you have the pleasure of eating this yummy hospital food?" he teased.

"Nope."

"Are you happy because you're driving my car while I'm laid up in here?"

"I haven't left the hospital at all, so no," I answered.

"So, what is it? Tell me, my love," he urged, a delicious smirk playing on his lips.

"I'm happy the man I love has come back to me. I can't wait until things are back to normal, including your crazy ways."

"What crazy ways?" he feigned innocence.

"You know exactly what I'm talking about. But never fear. I'm looking forward to the amazing make-up sex we'll have once we're done arguing." I gripped his hand and leaned in. "I can't wait until I have the opportunity to show you how much I've missed you."

His eyes sprung open like that was the last thing he expected me to say. *Well, I'm only human.* I would be a liar if I didn't admit Alek still did things to me, invading my brain with the naughtiest of thoughts, especially when he ran his tongue over his lips to moisten them before he spoke.

"The second we're home, I'm taking you to bed and we're not leaving for two weeks. That's the amount of time I've lost with you, so it's how much time I need to make this right."

I knew our separation killed him as much as it did me, but it was no one's fault. Okay...well, it was kind of his fault for lunging at Megan while she was holding a knife. But then again, I'd done the same thing when I'd been shot. Each of us was trying to protect the other, essentially protecting our own hearts.

We'd sure been through a lot during the course of our relationship, but I wouldn't change a thing if it meant we would always find our way back to each other.

I didn't want to burst his bubble, but I didn't want him getting ahead of himself either. "Alek, the doctor said it would be another week before you were able to go home, and once there, you have to take it easy until you're fully recovered. So, as much as I would love to spend weeks in bed with you, it won't be happening until I say you're able to do so. Got it?"

He looked annoyed but gave in. "Got it," he said, a wave of pain ripping through him and reminding him it was going to take some time to fully heal.

Even pouting, he was gorgeous.

~42~

Alek

I was finally being released from the hospital. The doctor thought I was well enough to go home and finish my recuperation there. I was going to need physical therapy to make sure I was functioning and moving at full capacity. Sara had already set everything up, asking for a male therapist to come in three times a week until he deemed me well enough to stop.

I asked her why she hadn't chosen a female therapist for me and she narrowed her eyes. Her jaw clenched, and I knew exactly why. She was about to give me a stern talking-to when I winked and she instantly relaxed, knowing I was simply teasing her.

"Do you have everything, Alek?" Sara gave the room a once-over before we headed out. I'd spent way too much time cooped up in there and I couldn't wait to breathe some goddamn fresh air.

"Yeah, babe, I'm good. Let's get the hell out of here already. I can't wait until we're home and we can start my therapy," I teased, slapping her ass. She squealed in surprise.

She turned around and crushed her body to mine, leaning up on her tippy-toes so she could press her gorgeous lips to mine. "Don't get cute, mister. We're not risking any further injury because we want to devour each other. Trust me, I know it's been a long time, but I refuse to be the reason why you don't fully recover."

"We'll see about that."

I took one step into the hallway when a nurse yelled at me. "Mr. Devera. You have to wait for the wheelchair. You can't just walk out."

"I'm fine. My legs aren't broken," I argued, attempting to take another step. I was a little more than aggravated, but Sara stopped me before I bit the woman's head off for simply doing her job.

"We'll wait for the chair," she said, pushing me back inside the room. As my mouth parted in protest, she whispered in my ear, "The sooner you follow the rules, Mr. Devera, the sooner you can claim my body as your own." She licked the tender part of my lobe before nipping it with her teeth.

I was instantly hard.

I threw my hands up in mock-surrender and waited for the damn wheelchair.

~~~~

The next three weeks flew by. Physical therapy kept me busy...and frustrated. Thankfully, Kael had a great head for business. I'd asked if he could oversee a few of my projects while I recuperated. He'd agreed with no hesitation.

Sara and I hadn't talked about *that* night. I couldn't bring myself to make her relive it. The only part I still struggle with is the fact I should have found out who Megan was way before I actually did. I didn't know why I let myself slip. Actually, I *did* know. I didn't want to push the issue so soon after Sara decided to give me another chance. Even though I eventually went behind her back anyway.

She was my life, my whole world, and there was nothing I wouldn't do to protect her. But never again would I ignore my gut feeling. She'd promised to never argue with me again about the big stuff.

The little stuff? Yeah, it was still going to be an uphill battle, but there were ways around it. I could be quite resourceful when I needed to be which, with her, was most of the time.

One day, toward the end of the day's therapy session, Sara strolled into the gym I'd set up. Michael, my therapist, was keeping a close watch over me as I used the treadmill. Thank God, too. As soon as she walked in, my eyes instantly found her and I almost lost my footing. Michael grabbed my arm to steady me and shook his head because he knew what caused me to falter. It'd happened quite often.

I was still experiencing some soreness in my stomach, an occurrence I thought would have dissipated weeks before. I knew as long as I still felt a twinge of pain, Sara wasn't going to let me touch her. I couldn't fake it either because she read it all over my face when I moved the wrong way.

She did her best not to tease me, but my cock instantly hardened whenever she was around. Shit, she didn't even need to be in the same room with me and I was throbbing. My imagination and memories were my worst enemies as of late.

"How much longer before I'm a hundred percent?" I asked, increasing the speed on the treadmill. I was determined to push myself toward the finish line.

Michael leaned over me, saw the speed, and punched the button to decrease it. "Longer if you keep pushing yourself too hard, Mr. Devera." He shot a displeased look my way as he wrote something down on that damn tablet of his.

"I don't understand why the fuck I'm still sore," I huffed, clenching my teeth in aggravation.

"Sometimes, our bodies are the ones to decide when enough is enough. And yours seems to be quite the stubborn one." When I shot him an annoyed look, he quickly faltered. "What I mean is you've been through quite an ordeal, and you can't expect to heal overnight. It takes as long as it takes."

"Overnight? Did you just say that to me? It's been almost a month since I've been home, doing everything you've told me. I've been resting when I'm supposed to, and doing this shit when I'm supposed to!" I yelled, waving at the mass amounts of equipment spread all over the room. Overly irate, I slammed my fist down on the treadmill, venting all my anger on the inanimate object.

"Alek, I know you're frustrated, but please don't take it out on Michael." Sara had walked up behind me when I was in the middle of my slight meltdown. I locked eyes with her for a full ten seconds before I jumped off the treadmill and slowly stalked her. She backed away, knowing full well what was going to happen if I caught her.

"Sara, come here," I coaxed.

"We're not alone, Alek. Stop it," she whispered, but she was weakening. I saw her glance back and forth between me and Michael, but I didn't care. She was mine, and I needed her warmth to calm me. And since I couldn't claim her like I wanted to, I would settle for the taste of her sweet lips.

Michael had been standing across the room, closer to Sara than I was. He approached her, his arm stretched out as if he was going to touch her.

He better not touch her. He better not touch her.

He fucking touched her.

"Are you okay, Sara?" he asked, his hand brushing over her upper arm. *What is going on?* He was acting a little too familiar with my woman and it pissed me off.

Before I even realized what was happening, my feet propelled me forward. I might not have been a hundred percent better, but I was well enough to kick his ass.

Sara saw me coming, took notice of his hand on her shoulder and suddenly looked slightly panicked. She knew what was coming and did her best to handle the situation before it spiraled out of control.

Moving a little to the right, his hand slipped away. "Yes. Thank you, Michael. I'm fine." She shot me a look as I breached the space between us, but no amount of silent pleading was going to stop me.

As I was about to reach out and throttle him, I heard him say, "Don't worry. Mr. Devera will be as good as new very soon. He's making so much progress already; it's only a matter of time." Michael still hadn't realized I was directly behind him. "I'm doing my best to make sure he doesn't overdo it, but maybe you could do your part, as well."

Both of us looked on in confusion.

"What do you mean?" she asked, perplexed.

Michael had the decency to realize what he'd said, but he continued on nonetheless. "It's my job as his therapist to ensure his whole being is in sync with itself. And sometimes..." He faltered for a quick second. "Sometimes, it means certain needs have to be met so he can give his all to fully recuperating."

I like where this is headed.

My anger had suddenly disappeared, smug satisfaction taking its place as I smirked at Sara. I'd been saying the same thing to her ever since I came home, but she ignored me, telling me it would do more harm than good. *Now that Michael said it, she'll have to take it more seriously.*

"I....I, uh...I don't know what you mean."

"We're all adults here," Michael responded. "Sex is the best way to release the endorphins, which is vital for a positive attitude. Which, in turn, translates to a quicker recovery." He took a step back and bumped into me. Giving me a faint smile, he finished with, "Don't worry. He's good enough for some light activity."

My cheeks hurt with how big my smile was.

"What are you grinning at?" She chuckled. I had to admit, seeing Sara slightly embarrassed was adorable.

"You heard the man, baby. And he knows what he's talking about." I breached the distance which separated us and pinned her against the wall. "I want to start the other part of my therapy. Right now." I crushed my mouth to hers before she could utter a word.

For once, she didn't fight me, knowing full well she needed me as much as I needed her.

Michael quickly gathered his things and left the room, not wanting to bear witness to what was about to happen, even though, in part, he had a hand in it. I had to make sure to give him a big raise.

~43~

Sara

I think my face was still red, but I never had any time to dwell on my reaction before Alek worked me into such a frenzy, I didn't think I would ever recover.

Pulling me from the room, he rushed me up the stairs then down the hallway to our bedroom. Once inside, he wrapped his arm around my waist and pulled me into his hungry embrace. "I've missed you more than you could possibly know. Finally," he exhaled, "I've been given the green light to make you scream." He toyed with my lips, running his warm tongue over the top of them, stopping once in a while to nibble on me as if I was his afternoon snack.

When I tried to deepen the kiss, he suddenly backed away.

"What are you doing?" I panted. I was already squirming where I stood, an intense ache spreading all over my body as he continued to stare at me.

"I'm only doing to you what you've done to me for weeks."

"You're purposely teasing me?" I pouted. "What I did was because of your health." I retreated, his eyes intently following me.

"Are you upset, sweetheart?" he asked, still confused as to why I was putting distance between us.

"No," I said, a little too blasé. "I can always take care of myself." Fiddling with the hem of my dress, I said, "Do you want to watch?" Knowing Alek loved to watch me touch myself, I heard him gasp at my brazen tone. Surely, he thought he'd had the upper hand. Clearly, he was wrong. Pulling up the bottom of my dress, I first exposed my white lace panties. His eyes widened. Drawing the material up further, I flashed my taut stomach then my matching bra. A garbled sound erupted from his throat, his satisfaction clear in the way he admired me. Finally, I hoisted the damn thing over my head and tossed it to the side, standing in front of him and waiting to see what would happen next.

"What now?" he groaned, adjusting himself through his workout shorts.

Never taking my eyes off him, I slipped my fingers under the lace material and slowly rubbed myself. "Are you going to make me finish myself off?" My hips bucked forward as a small gasp fell from my lips.

Knowing it wouldn't be long until he gave in, he removed his shirt and shorts until he was standing in front of me with nothing but his boxer briefs on. The outline of his steel cock made my mouth water. All of my attention was fixated on him as I continued to stroke myself into oblivion.

"Goddamn it!" he shouted. "You're so fucking sexy." He licked his lips as he rid himself of his last piece of clothing. Stepping toward me, he fisted his arousal and began stroking himself. Slowly. He knew what he was doing to me, as I knew what I was doing to him.

Our little dance only continued for another thirty seconds before he was on me. Tearing my hand from my panties, he drew my fingers into his mouth. "You taste like heaven," he moaned, sucking my essence from me. "I don't want to play anymore," he confessed. "You win."

I smiled in victory as I took his hand and led him toward the bed.

Gently pushing him onto his back, he fought me until I shook my head. We were going to have sex my way or no way at all. A mere glance into my eyes told him so.

"We're not going to fuck tonight, Alek. We're going to make love. Slow and gentle." Straddling his waist, I leaned down until my lips took his in a sensual kiss. His tongue swirled with mine as I moaned into his mouth. "Can you do that for me?" I asked.

"Not if you keep bouncing on top of my dick." I hadn't even realized I was squirming around until he called me out on it.

His hands grasped my waist as he tried to raise me up enough to hover over the tip of him.

"Alek," I warned. "Let me do all the work."

"I'm not going to fucking break, Sara." Irritation flashed across his face but was quickly erased when I freed my breasts from my lacy bra. I tossed it aside as he pulled me lower. He latched onto a nipple as his hand tweaked the other. The sucking sensation shot a bolt of pleasure straight through me.

Everything was going exactly the way I'd planned until he pushed me back upright, ripped off my panties in one swipe, clutched my hips and tried once more to position me over him.

I slapped his hands away immediately and tried to move off him. "What the hell?" he asked, feigning injury. "Where do you think you're going?"

"You have to agree to let me take charge, Alek. Agree, or this doesn't happen tonight."

"Fine," he huffed. "I'll let you do the work this time. But I'm going to sample my dessert before you serve me the main course." A sly smile graced his mouth as he said, "Since you don't want me to exert myself, you're going to have move forward so I can taste you." Pulling me up his body, he helped to position me directly over his hungry mouth.

Placing my hands on the headboard to keep me steady, I rocked back and forth over his face. His hands gripped my ass as he drove his tongue inside me. My hand fell and tangled up in his hair, forcing his mouth even closer. "Please, don't stop," I cried.

The pressure was building, so intense I almost pulled away from his sweet torture. As my breathing changed, I felt him smile, his lips latching onto my clit.

"Come on my tongue, baby. Let me taste you."

And I did. I came so hard my legs shook while my vision blurred. As my orgasm racked through me, I held my breath, simply forgetting to breathe.

As I moved back down his body, I captured his lips with mine, tasting remnants of my release on his tongue.

"Now it's my turn to bring you pleasure."

"You bring me pleasure every second you agree to be mine, Sara."

He was being so sweet, but I didn't want sweet right then. I wanted him to bury himself inside me, pushing me to ride him until he screamed out *my* name.

Leaning over, I grabbed a condom from the nightstand, ripped off the wrapper and sheathed him in three seconds flat.

Taking hold, I whispered, "I love you," as I took in every inch of him.

There was a brief moment of discomfort because we hadn't had sex in what seemed like forever. Plus, it always took me some time to adjust to the sheer girth of him.

Finally, I was able to move. "Do you like that?" I asked, rising slowly until he was almost all the way out, then slamming back down as I swiveled my hips around.

"I fucking love it. But I fear I'm going to explode sooner than I want to if you keep doing that." He was so caught up in the moment, he tried to raise himself to take my nipple into his mouth.

Of course, I scolded him.

"Alek, don't."

"Why? You love it when I do that." He looked confused, until I explained why I'd reprimanded him.

"I do. But let me come to you."

"Oh, for Christ's sake. Are you serious?" He laughed, but I could tell he was annoyed I was treating him as if he would shatter.

"Yes, and if you don't listen to me, I'll leave you to finish yourself off." We were involved in one heated staring contest. "Do you understand me?"

There was no way he wanted to give in, but I could tell he knew it was the lesser of two evils. "Fine," he relented.

"Good." My hands covered my breasts, playing with my nipples until they pebbled from my touch. "Are these what you want?"

"You know I do. Now, stop torturing me before I flip you on your back and overexert myself by fucking you senseless."

As he teased me, I made love to my man.

Nice and slow.

Only once since my final warning did he try and switch up the pace, but he quickly slowed, giving me back the control I demanded. I nibbled his lips as I continued to ride him, swallowing his grunts as he toed the fine line of destruction.

"Come with me, Sara. Come with me now."

I sat up straighter, placed his hands on my breasts and brought it home.

For the both of us.

~44~

Sara

My body was perfectly molded to his, his strong arms wrapping around me as he snuggled in close behind me.

"Sara," he whispered, his breath cascading over the shell of my ear. He was already starting to harden, his excitement pressing into the small of my back.

"Yes," I mumbled, tired from hours of slow and torturous lovemaking.

"Let's get married." As soon as the words were spoken, he placed his hand on my waist and turned me over, giving me no choice but to look at him.

Is he serious?

"Are you serious?" I asked, stricken dumb with shock.

He smirked. Typical Alek fashion. "Not the response I was looking for, but I'll go with it." He placed a sweet kiss on my lips before pulling back. "Yes, I'm serious."

I sat up in bed, needing to prepare for the conversation we were going to have. "But we haven't even lived together that long."

"So?"

"So, don't you think we're rushing?" I fiddled with the sheets which covered my lap. My bare breasts were in full view for him to enjoy, but they did nothing to distract him from continuing his sudden topic of conversation.

"Not at all. I know I want to spend the rest of my life with you." He pulled me back down on the bed, positioning me so I was lying on top of him. "Do you want to spend the rest of your life with me?" Why did he look so worried I was going to say no? Running my hand along his jaw, his stubble tickled my palm. I looked into his beautiful green eyes and told him the absolute truth.

"I do," I confirmed. *Funny choice of words.*

"Then what's the problem?" He held his breath, waiting for me to answer. I think he assumed I was going to argue with him, or stubbornly point out the reasons we shouldn't charge head-on into such a big commitment. But I had nothing. He was totally right. Why were we waiting?

"There is no problem," I said, tangling my fingers in his hair. My tongue pushed against his luscious lips, asking for permission to taste him. It was granted immediately. His need for me intensified the longer our mouths dueled for ownership. When I thought he was going to push inside me, he pulled back and hopped off the bed.

Reaching for me, he grabbed my hand and tugged for me to stand in front of him.

"Stay here," he demanded, giving me another quick kiss before he disappeared into his closet. He reappeared, stalking toward me as if I was his very lifeline and he needed to touch me in order to stay alive. In his hand was a small, black jewelry box. "I'm going to do this officially." He laughed, suddenly becoming nervous.

Slowly, he lowered himself until he was on one knee. Taking my left hand in his, he professed his undying love for me. "Sara, baby. I've loved you for what seems like forever. The day I walked into your shop was the first day of the rest of my life. I know it may sound cliché, but it's absolutely true. Your love has made me a better man. Every day, I try and show you how much you mean to me, and I'll keep trying until I take my last breath." Blowing out an anxious breath, he asked, "Sara Nicole Hawthorne, will you do me the honor of becoming my wife?"

As he looked up at me, a pensive look in his eye with each second that slipped by in silence, I fell even more in love with him. I'd waited my entire life for him, and I wasn't going to go another day without letting everyone know how much we were destined to be together.

A tear fell down my cheek as I answered him. "Yes. Yes, I'll marry you." He shot to his feet and crushed me against his body, raining kisses all over my face. Finally, he stepped back, removed the ring from its box and placed it on my finger.

The sheer size of it made me nervous. How the hell did he expect me to wear something so large on my hand and be confident someone wasn't going to bop me over the head and steal it?

"I know it's overwhelming, but do you like it?" He was still nervous, and I found it rather endearing. Alek Devera wasn't a man who showed his vulnerable side too often, but when he did, my heart ached to love him that much more.

"I love it," I answered honestly. "But you're going to have to insure this bad boy," I teased. "It's huge."

"Already taken care of, sweetheart."

As we laid in bed, limbs gloriously tangled together, I couldn't help but feel truly blessed. I'd found the man of my dreams, and although we'd definitely had our ups and downs, I wouldn't trade a second of it.

Falling asleep that night was different. A peace settled over me I hadn't even realized was missing. My entire life had been leading up to that moment, and the many more to come for us.

He and I.

Lovers and friends.

Soon to be husband and wife.

Epilogue

As I stood hovering over the bathroom sink, I was reminded of the time I'd anxiously waited to see if my future was going to change or not.

I'd been feeling off the past couple of weeks, exhaustion and nausea being the two main differences. I chalked it up to the long hours working at the shop, mixed with the stress of an ever-expanding business. I'd finally purchased the space next to Full Bloom, growing into a much more prosperous flower shop.

My cell rang, pulling me from my nervous thoughts. I didn't want to move until the results showed on the pregnancy test, but the persistent ringing gave me no choice.

Slowly moving toward my bed, I snatched up the phone and answered. "Hello?"

"Hey, honey. I'm calling to tell you I'm on my way home now. My meeting ended earlier than planned. Did you want me to pick you up anything on the way?"

I wasn't expecting him for another hour. A sudden wave of nausea washed over me as he waited for me to answer him. Breathing deeply through my nose, I calmed my stomach enough to speak. "No, I'm okay. But thank you."

Sensing there might be something wrong, he prodded me for more information. "Are you all right, Sara? You sound as if something is bothering you."

He was so attuned to me it was scary. A simple change in my voice or the slightest look gave away all my secrets, but only to the man who knew me best.

"I'm fine," I lied. "I'll see you soon."

After ending the call, I headed back toward the bathroom. I stood on the threshold, not sure if I was ready to check the results yet. Last time, Alexa happened to come home and discovered my panic. She stayed with me the whole time, offering me her strength as I found out if I was pregnant or not.

Thankfully, I wasn't.

Standing there all alone, I didn't know what to make of what I was feeling. I wasn't panicked like I was last time. Not even close. But I wasn't sure if I was hopeful, either.

A lot had changed in my life to cause me to reflect on what was really important. Family and friends were at the top of my list.

Alek had officially become my family a year before. The question was did I want to expand our circle of two? We'd talked about it on a few occasions. He never pushed, except when he groaned about still having to wear a condom while having sex with his wife. A simple look from me and he would cover up with no more complaints.

Finally taking a step into the bathroom, I picked up the test and stared at it. Re-reading the directions for the hundredth time, there was no doubt what the results were.

"Sara?" Alek called out. "Where are you?"

"Up here," I yelled back. I quickly stashed the test in the vanity drawer. I would tell him about it later, when we had time to really talk.

Alek strode in the room and took my breath away, as usual. Dressed in one of his designer suits, he looked beyond handsome. His hair was perfectly styled in his typical, purposely unruly way. A light stubble caressed his jaw, the look instantly reminding me of how it felt between my thighs earlier that morning.

As he stepped closer, I noticed one arm was resting behind his back. "Hi, beautiful." He leaned in and gave me a sweet kiss.

"Hi, yourself." Trying to peer around him, he moved every time I did. "What do you have behind your back?"

"Your anniversary present."

"Alek, we said we weren't going to exchange presents. That our love was—" He cut me off before I could finish.

"Our love is enough, but there was no way I wasn't buying my wife a gift on our first wedding anniversary." I walked away and disappeared into the closet. "Sara, come back here. Don't be mad."

Reappearing in front of him, I held my gift behind my back. "I knew you were going to ignore the rule. So, I did as well."

"You know you didn't have to do that, baby. Your love really *is* enough for me."

"Yeah, yeah," I teased. "Who wants to go first?" I asked, suddenly becoming nervous.

"Ladies first."

I brought my hand around to the front of me and handed him my gift. Watching his face as he opened it was nerve-racking. It wasn't anything worth monetary value. Would he like it? Would he understand the significance of it?

Before I could succumb to my frantic nerves, he ripped the paper off, turned it over and stared at his present. He was silent. I scanned his face to see his reaction but he was expressionless. Until I noticed his eyes suddenly became glassy. I knew he recognized the sentimental value of what I'd given him.

"Do you remember it?" I asked, my own emotions almost becoming too much.

He looked up and smiled. "Yes. It was the picture your grandmother had of you in her room. This," he said, holding the frame in the air, "was the first time I ever saw you." He'd become overwhelmed at my simple but meaningful present, and it made my heart soar.

So there *was* something I could give the man who had everything.

"Did you have it the whole time?" He continued to stare at it in disbelief.

"I did, but I didn't know it. I was going through some of my gram's things a while back and came across it. As soon as I found it, I knew I was going to give it to you for our anniversary. I hoped you'd like it." I smiled as he pulled me close.

"I love it. It's the best present I've ever received. Ever," he repeated.

Before he made me cry, his eyes still overcome with emotion, I asked, "Is it my turn now?"

"Yes, of course. Please, let me know if you don't like it. I can return it and pick something else."

"Hand it over, Mr. Devera," I demanded. He brought the gift around and placed it in my hand.

"Do you think you could call me that later tonight? In bed?" He laughed.

"Call you what? Mr. Devera?" When he only laughed harder, I couldn't distinguish if he was serious or not.

Pulling my attention back to the surprise in my hand, I slowly opened the box until my eyes feasted on a gorgeous diamond pendant, in the shape of a heart. "Alek, it's so beautiful," I gushed. The stone was large, but not so much it detracted from the flawless beauty of the necklace. When I turned it over, I saw he had something engraved into the back of it.

> *To my heart, my love and my soulmate. I'll love you forever.*

"It's nothing compared to what you just gave me, but I thought you would like it."

Cupping his cheek, I assured him his gift to me was as touching. He thought of me as he shopped for my present, knowing me so well, he'd been able to pick the perfect gift. "This is the best present anyone has ever given me. Ever," I said, squeezing his hand in mine.

"Even better than the Audi?" He was teasing me and I knew it.

"Even better than the Audi," I answered, giving him a quick kiss before placing the necklace on my dresser. I was going to wear it that evening, and I wanted it out in the open to gaze at while I dressed.

~~~~

After a fantastic dinner out, we made our way to Throttle for a quick drink before returning home, no doubt to engage in a night of ecstasy.

We were heading through the crowd when we spotted Matt, sitting at the bar. He looked to be alone, but there were so many people around him, it was hard to tell. As the crowd shifted, I took notice of a beautiful woman walking toward my dear friend. She smiled brightly as she drew near. Who was she? When I looked back to Matt, I noticed he was just as happy to see her.

Then they kissed.

And it wasn't platonic. Even from where I was standing, I picked up on the sexual heat passing between them. *What the hell?*

"Sara? Did you hear me?"

I was too wrapped up in the scene unfolding in front of me to even answer. Looking to see what drew my attention, he saw Matt, but their embrace had already ended.

"Matt's here. Can we say hi really quick before we sit down?" My curiosity was getting the better of me.

"Sure." Alek entwined his fingers with mine as we walked toward him and his mystery woman.

He saw us approaching and smiled. Big. Whoever she was had certainly put my dear friend in a great mood. *I think I like her.*

"Sara," he greeted, standing from his seat and giving me a kiss on the cheek. He then turned toward Alek and they shook hands. Thankfully, they had become friendly with one another, even grabbing the occasional beer now and again.

Matt glanced to the woman on his right, then back to us, before saying, "Sara. Alek. This is Isabelle." We exchanged greetings. Okay, so I knew her name, but who was she to Matt?

Alek handed me a drink as I decided to find out what was going on. "So, tell me, Isabelle. How do you know Matt?"

There was no hesitation when she answered. "I'm his fiancée."

The words hadn't even registered in my brain as Alek choked on his drink. Looking to me to see if it was a joke, I told him I knew as much as he did with a simple shrug.

"I KNEW it!" Alek shouted, pointing a finger in Matt's direction. "I knew you weren't gay!"

"What?" Matt exclaimed. Looking back and forth between the two of us, he was thoroughly confused himself. "You thought I was gay?" Before I could even answer him, he blurted out, "I'm not gay. I'll show you right now I'm not gay."

"Hey," Alek grunted. "Watch it." He was smirking, but there was a serious tone to his words.

How could I have been so off the mark? "Can I talk to you for a second?" I asked, grabbing his hand and pulling him through the crowd before he even had a chance to answer me.

Placing my untouched drink on a nearby table, I dove right in. "What's going on? Who is Isabelle? How long have you known her, Matt? And why didn't I know you had a freaking fiancée?" I fired off question after question, fully expecting an answer for each one of them.

"It's complicated, Sara," was all he said as he ran his fingers through his hair.

"Really? Can you give me a little more than *it's complicated?*"

"Not before you tell me why you thought I was gay!"

Sudden embarrassment crept over me as I fumbled to find the right words. "Well, for starters, women hit on you all the time, yet I've never known you to show any interest. Then there's the way I would catch you looking at other men."

"And what way was that, pray tell?"

"I don't know exactly. It was the way you huddled close while talking to them, or the way you watched them." His inquisitive stare made me nervous for some reason.

"Sara," he started, "I never showed any interest in other women because my heart belonged to someone else. Isabelle. She was the only one for me, and even though we hadn't been together in years, I still couldn't bring myself to be with somebody else. And as for *the way I watched other guys,* you obviously read into something which wasn't there." Huffing out a quick breath, he finished what he had to say. "I miss my friends back home. I was simply looking for someone to hang out with, you know, someone to do some male-bonding with. With our clothes on, of course." He was making fun of me and I didn't blame him.

"So...what's the story with Isabelle then?" I wanted to know more about the woman who had my friend all twisted-up.

"That's a story better told another day. When we have more time." When he saw how disappointed I was, he threw me a bone. "We dated all throughout high school, but some stuff happened, we broke up and I moved here, to Seattle, to escape everything."

I knew no matter how much I pushed, he wasn't going to reveal his whole life story in the middle of a crowded club.

So I left it alone.

After saying our goodbyes, we headed back home. It was definitely going to be a long night because there was something else I needed to talk to my husband about.

~~~~

Moving toward the bed, I held the pregnancy test behind my back as I approached. Alek was already lying down, watching me, the desire he held for me written all over his face.

Crawling on top of the covers, I moved as close to him as I could while still maintaining some necessary distance. "Alek, I have something I need to talk to you about." The look on my face told him I was serious.

Instant worry stole his previous expression. "What is it? What's wrong?" He noticed I was hiding something behind me and he moved to pull me close, his impatience heightening my worry. "Show me what you have in your hand, Sara."

I never said a word as I handed him the test. I nervously bit my lip, not quite sure what to say to him.

"Is this what I think it is?" he asked, a hopeful look in his eye. "Does this plus sign mean you're pregnant?"

I nodded.

I didn't know what else to do.

I'd been trying to come to grips with what those results meant all night.

"But how?" he questioned. "We've been using protection this whole time.

"Well...not the time in the shower last month. Remember? When you pulled out?" I smiled as the memory dawned on him. "Apparently, that method of birth control is not so effective."

"I guess not," he smiled. Quickly taking on a more serious look, he asked, "How do you feel about it?" I hated he hampered his excitement at the news of me being pregnant. But being the wonderful man he was, he was more worried about my well-being than his own enthusiasm.

"I've been thinking about it all evening, and I think I'm...happy." A small smile tipped my lips as I voiced my thoughts again. "Yeah, I'm happy about it."

What had threatened me the most over the years wasn't Samuel, or even his sister. It was the fear something bad was always lurking around the corner. Being too engrossed in that way of thinking blocks out all the good life has to offer.

"So, we're going to have a baby?" he practically sang.

"Yes. We're going to have a baby." Although the words sounded foreign to me, I was happier each time I said them.

As I laid my head on his chest later that evening, hearing his heart beat in sync with my own, I traced the scar on his stomach. Without even realizing he was doing it, his finger found the one on my shoulder. While our fingertips danced over the puckered skin, I couldn't help but think.

We both bore the scars of my past while our future grew inside me.

The End

Acknowledgements

Thank you to my husband for being patient with me as I released one book after another, spending countless hours locked away in my office. Thank you for giving me the time I needed to get these characters out of my head and onto paper. I love you!

A huge thank you to my family and friends for your continued love and support. I don't know what I would do without you!

To the ladies at Hot Tree Editing, I can't say enough great things about you. You continue to amaze me and I can't wait until our next project together. You have been truly fantastic!

I would also like to thank Clarise at CT Cover Creations. Your work speaks for itself. I'm absolutely thrilled with the book covers for this trilogy. They are beyond gorgeous!

To Beth, the best PA ever! Your love and support is truly priceless. I'm beyond thrilled we've become such dear friends. I don't know what I would do without you, woman!

To all of the bloggers who have shared my work, I'm forever indebted to you. You ladies are simply wonderful!

To all of you who have reached out to me to let me know how much you loved the first two books in the Addicted Trilogy, and are anxiously biting your nails for their conclusion...here you go. Enjoy!

And last but not least, I would like to thank you, the reader. I hope you enjoy the final installment of Alek and Sara's story.

About the Author

S. Nelson grew up with a love of reading and a very active imagination, never putting pen to paper, or fingers to keyboard until two years ago.

When she isn't engrossed in creating one of the many stories rattling around inside her head, she loves to read and travel as much as she can.

She lives in Pennsylvania with her husband and two dogs, enjoying the ever changing seasons.

If you would like to follow or contact her please do so at the follow:

Email Address: snelsonauthor8@gmail.com

Facebook: https://www.facebook.com/pages/S-Nelson/630474467061217?ref=hl

Goodreads: https://www.goodreads.com/author/show/12897502.S_Nelson

Amazon: http://www.amazon.com/S.-Nelson/e/B00T6RIQIQ/ref=ntt_athr_dp_pel_1

Made in the USA
Middletown, DE
14 September 2017